# Earth

## to

# Charlie

## JUSTIN OLSON

SIMON & SCHUSTER BFYR

NEW YORK   LONDON   TORONTO   SYDNEY   NEW DELHI

*To those who look up*

SIMON & SCHUSTER BFYR

An imprint of Simon & Schuster Children's Publishing Division
1230 Avenue of the Americas, New York, New York 10020

SIMON & SCHUSTER BFYR is a trademark of Simon & Schuster, Inc.
For information about special discounts for bulk purchases, please contact Simon
& Schuster Special Sales at 1-866-506-1949 or business@simonandschuster.com.
The Simon & Schuster Speakers Bureau can bring authors to your live event. For
more information or to book an event, contact the Simon & Schuster Speakers
Bureau at 1-866-248-3049 or visit our website at www.simonspeakers.com.
Also available in a SIMON & SCHUSTER BFYR hardcover edition
Cover design by Krista Vossen
The text for this book was set in Minion Pro.
Manufactured in the United States of America
First SIMON & SCHUSTER BFYR paperback edition April 2020
2  4  6  8  10  9  7  5  3  1

The Library of Congress has cataloged the hardcover edition as follows:
Names: Olson, Justin, 1986– author.
Title: Earth to Charlie / Justin Olson.
Description: First edition. | New York : Simon & Schuster Books for Young
Readers, [2019] | Summary: After his mother's disappearance,
Charlie became a bullied loner, obsessed with UFO sightings, so when
new student Seth wants to be his friend, Charlie is suspicious.
Identifiers: LCCN 2017046570 | ISBN 9781534419520 (hardcover) |
ISBN 9781534419537 (pbk) | ISBN 9781534419544 (eBook)
Subjects: | CYAC: Friendship—Fiction. | Bullies—Fiction. |
High schools—Fiction. | Schools—Fiction. | Alien abduction—Fiction. |
Single-parent families—Fiction.
Classification: LCC PZ7.1.O4863 Ear 2019 | DDC [Fic]—dc23
LC record available at https://lccn.loc.gov/2017046570

When it's all over, desire doesn't die.

—Karen Fiser

# PART ONE

## ZEROING IN ON THE INFINITE

# THE GREAT WHITE SHOCK

•••••

My mind drifts from one thought to the next. My bed-sheets are finally warm. I roll to one side, then to the other. After a bit of adjusting, I find myself on my back. My eyes shut.

I wait restlessly for sleep to find me.

The house is so deadened of people and activity that the air feels heavy and stagnant. If someone were to walk into my room right now, they'd think it was a tomb.

And I, the body.

Lying here, I think of this time when I was five, and my mom was watching me in front of our house. I was riding my tricycle on the sidewalk, and I flew past her and shouted, "I'm flying!" I always believed I was a plane pilot on my tricycle, and later on my bike. But I've outgrown make-believe.

I rode back, and she smiled, her perfect white teeth showing in the bright sun, the bandana holding her wild hair in place, and she pointed up. She said, "You were in the sky, Charlie. You're the best pilot in the world."

I laughed and repeated, "I'm the best pilot in the world!" I pedaled down the road, before turning my tricycle around to face her.

I stared at the road—the imaginary runway—as it continued on in front of me for what seemed like forever.

My flashback is cut short when I hear a large buzz coming from outside my window. It sounds electric—like a weed-eater. Only, it's so loud that I have to cover my ears. But the buzz is secondary to the light, which flashes so brightly I'm momentarily blinded.

I sit up with a start and see the white light dissipate as rapidly as it arrived. I grab my glasses on the nightstand, and within a half second I am at my window, pulling up the blinds and staring out across the night sky. I see nothing, but that doesn't stop me from darting out of my room, down the wooden stairs, and out the back patio door. My bare feet feel cold as I run through the blades of grass. The night air cools my arms and legs too. But I have to run after that light. I have to follow it, and when I make it to the edge of my yard, I realize I am trapped by our chain-link fence. Standing there, under the crystal clear sky, I worry that the light is long gone.

Then again, it might have landed somewhere near me, in the forest.

As this is the first time—and might be the only time—I've witnessed a likely UFO encounter, I have no choice but to chase it.

I bolt inside and run up the stairs for my shoes and hoodie.

I flip on my bedroom light and see the mess that is

my bedroom. The floor is a swirl of clothes, magazines, books, more clothes. I look for my socks but can't find any. "Come on!"

There's one white sock under a sweater. I toss books aside and find a black sock. It'll have to work. Time isn't on my side, and I'm getting frustrated.

I grab a sweater, which says WHITEHALL HIGH TROJANS on the front in purple letters, with a purple armored helmet underneath. I hate this sweater, but it's the only one within reach. As I turn to my door, there's a silhouette blocking my escape.

"What in the Lord's name are you doing? You should be in bed." Even five feet away, I smell the beer on his breath and clothes.

"I have to . . ." I can't tell him.

Not moving from the door, my dad seems like he gives zero shits about my frantic pace.

"I need to go!" I say. "I'll be back soon." Though, I hope that's not true.

"It's a school night, Charlie. You're not going anywhere."

My dad, even drunk, can enforce his parental responsibilities. He works at the Golden Sunlight Mine and always has a five-o'clock shadow and dirt under his fingernails. His clothes always look like they should've been shredded into rags years ago.

I bounce on the balls of my feet. "Come on, Dad. Please!"

This is a matter of life and death, after all.

Moseying into my room as if he has all the time in the world, he says, "This better not be about some UFO nonsense."

I notice that as my dad approaches me, my door is left wide open, so I dart past him. But I trip on a pile of clothes, and the next thing I know, I'm facedown on the floor. I roll over, and my dad is towering above me like a giant.

My heart beats heavily at the thought of the UFO flying away.

Leaving me here.

I just stare at my dad. He makes no effort to help me up. Instead he walks to my window and searches the sky. "Nope. Nothing out there. Nothing ever out there." The blinds hit the windowsill with a definite thud. He lets go of the string and steps over me and heads to the door.

"Get to bed. But I'm glad to see you're wearing your birthday present." He starts to close my door but then stops. "And you know better than to try to run away like that. What has gotten into you?" My bedroom door slams shut, and my world shakes. I sit on the floor, unable to chase after the one thing that came to save me. Though, my search is far from over.

# MY HISTORY

• • • • •

I am wide awake because I've let the one and only thing I've spent years trying to find escape. Why did I let it get away so easily? Why didn't I just leave my room after my dad went to bed? I have squandered the greatest opportunity of my short, pathetic life—the opportunity to finally be reunited with my mother.

I toss and turn in bed and try to calm my mind. I think about the moments that led me to this night.

I started scanning the sky in seventh grade, the night after she disappeared, and I used binoculars in my bedroom. On the first night of searching, I saw something moving and blinking. I got so excited that I jumped up and down. My search for aliens had been almost too easy. But when I put the binoculars back up to the sky, I could no longer find the blinking light.

The following night, at about the same time, I saw the same blinking light in roughly the same place. That was when I knew something was wrong. What I had been focusing on was too steady, too noticeable. It dawned on me: a satellite. My shoulders slumped in defeat.

As I kept searching, I realized that binoculars were not helpful. It's too hard to see anything with them in the dark, and they started giving me a headache. Besides, if a UFO were near, would I even need binoculars?

I began to leave the house to search the night sky. While I loved the unobstructed view, I missed my second-story vantage point. So I started hiking into the woods and up onto a hill not too far from my house. But my dad got suspicious that I was searching for UFOs, and he told me I couldn't go into the woods at night anymore (but he was rarely around to enforce his rule so I just made sure I was home before him).

I've also spent hours upon hours looking up UFOs online, so I know what to watch out for. Of course there's the usual spacecraft: discs, saucers, pretty much what we see in alien films. They are usually gray or black. But there are also some weird UFO shapes that you'd never really consider: pyramids/triangles, bowls, spheres, and oblong shapes. That's just scratching the surface. Until tonight I hadn't personally seen a UFO. At least what I would assume is a UFO. Maybe there's one right outside my house, and I can't see it. Or it has disguised itself as something else . . . like a satellite. . . . But I really don't think about that kind of stuff, or I'd get depressed and paranoid, knowing they're so close and still so out-of-reach.

It's now the dead of night, and I yawn, stretching my body, but I can't will myself to close my eyes. I wonder if Meridian X saw this.

The summer of my eighth-grade year, I drew a map

of the stars. It wasn't a great map, but it took weeks to draw, as I had to keep looking up. I broke up the sky into segments so that I could search each grid more in depth for UFOs and mark each section off as I went. Only problem? The earth rotates and the sky changes—the stars are constantly dancing and jumping, and planets are coming in and out of view. So by the time I was done with one section of the sky, the entire sky had shifted, and I quickly saw the futility of my endeavor.

Maybe all this sounds so simple and obvious, but I didn't know anything when I started. It was my own learning experience.

Now I get up and go to my bedroom window. I look up—knowing so little about the vastness above me and feeling small and insignificant.

How could I have just let the UFO get away?

# IT WAS THE BEST OF TIMES . . . BUT MOSTLY IT WAS THE WORST OF TIMES

. . . . .

As I head down the oppressive school hallway to Ms. Monakey's room for first period on the last week of school, I hear, "Write anything today, Charles DICK-ens?" Joey turns to his two idiot friends, Matt and Psych, and laughs. They always sound like a bunch of donkeys when they laugh, which is why I've dubbed them the Ass Trio. Oh, and they're assholes. That's why too.

This is just one of the many jabs I hear throughout the course of a given school day. It actually amazes me that these Neanderthals still get pleasure out of such stale material. I ignore them and continue on.

I believe that my parents set me up for constant bullying, though I have come to believe it wasn't on purpose—which has kept me from hating them.

See, my name is Charlie Dickens. It's not "Charles"—like the famous author. Even my birth certificate says "Charlie."

The first day I came home in a rather sour mood was in

third grade, because I had been teased about my name. My mom told me that even as a little girl she had dreamed of having a boy named Charlie. Even back when her maiden name was Severson. I had no problem with my first name.

The problem came because my dad's last name is Dickens.

I don't think either one of my parents had read a Charles Dickens novel in their lives. Though, they had to have at least heard the name. Had to have known about him. So how either one didn't put two and two together, I do not know. And their lack of forethought has haunted me to this day.

Okay . . . so the story isn't so cut-and-dried (like most decent stories). My mom had been told up until the day I was born that she was having a girl. So when out popped a boy, her eyes lit up and she said, after having been in labor for ten and a half hours, "It's my own baby Charlie."

Little Charlie Dickens. That name—those two words—have trapped me, and will forever.

I'm sitting in Ms. Monakey's classroom waiting for the bell to ring. There's this website called Montana UFO Sightings. (Original, right?) It's maintained by a woman who calls herself Meridian X, who lives in Butte—a town about thirty miles west of here. I'm checking to see if there are any reports of UFOs from last night in the Whitehall area. I need to find some validation.

As last night grew longer, I began to convince myself that I was crazy for thinking I'd seen a UFO. How could my dad not have heard the noise or seen the explosion of white light?

Did I make it up?

Did I actually fall asleep and dream it?

I see no new activity on the website, which doesn't mean last night's event didn't happen. It could just mean that Meridian X is slow at updating a website that looks like it was made in the early 2000s.

Next thing I know, someone's hot breath is tickling the hairs on my neck. I assume it's some jerk trying to be funny, and I turn to see the new kid leaning over the desk behind me. "There's really a website for Montana UFO sightings?"

I quickly exit out of the internet browser and feel my face grow warm. I shouldn't be so careless. "Mind your own business."

Okay, so not the most welcoming sentence, but after years of constant teasing, I'm always on guard.

"Sorry. Just trying to make conversation." The new kid's name is Seth, and he leans back in his chair and pulls out his phone.

I adjust my glasses and then decide to ask, since there really are only a couple of people in the classroom, and none are paying attention to us. "Were you awake around midnight last night?"

"Shouldn't I mind my own business?"

"Sorry. I thought you were going to make fun of me or something. That's why I said that. I'm just wondering if you happened to hear a loud buzz or a see a white light?"

Seth's eyebrows draw in, and his lips purse together. "Hmmm. You know, I think I did. But I think it was just a semi or something, and I had headphones on."

"Really?" This was great validation.

Well, sort of validation.

"Do you believe it was a UFO? Is that why you were on that site?" he asks.

Not wanting him to tease me, I shrug. "Doubt it." Though, it's only a matter of time before he gets the memo and starts teasing me anyway. Or realizes on his own that I am the school's outcast. But to be honest, it feels oddly safer to be alone and wrapped in a cocoon of my own making.

First period Spanish is the only class I have with the new kid, which means he's not a freshman like me. But the school is small enough that I see everyone all the time. Unfortunately. I even see those I never want to see another day of my life (like the Ass Trio). I've noticed that the new kid has worn a camera around his neck every day. It looks like one of those expensive professional-photographer cameras. It's actually pretty sweet.

The bell rings, and Ms. Monakey stands in front of the room and clasps her hands together. "All right, class. *¿Están listos?* Let's begin."

But between a possible UFO sighting and talking to the new kid, my mind is too distracted to pay attention. I'm wondering why Seth moved to Whitehall so close to the end of the school year, but it's really none of my business, is it? This is all I know about him, from his first day in class, nearly two weeks ago:

Ms. Monakey asked him to come to the front of the room. She said, "*Este es Seth. Seth es nuevo aquí.*" She looked at him. "Do you want to tell us a little about yourself?"

Seth looked around the room and lingered a second on

my eyes before saying, "*Oui*. My name is Seth. Seth is new here." He chuckled. "Just kidding. I'm from—"

Ms. Monakey corrected him, "*Soy de.*"

"Oh, right. *Soy de* Miles City."

"*¡Maravilloso!*"

"No. Terrible. *Muy mal.* I was hoping Whitehall would have fewer rednecks than Miles City, which should be easy for any city to achieve. But so far I've been woefully disappointed." He went to sit down, but stopped. "Oh, and . . . *Yo amo fotografía.*" He held up his camera. "And trashy *televisión.*"

As he passed by my desk, I felt like he looked at me again and held my gaze a little longer. It was uncomfortable, but maybe I'm just not used to positive attention at school.

# FORGETFUL ELOISE
# IS STILL ALIVE

......

My grandmother lives in a room about the size of two regular-size closets. Not only is it small, but it's as bland as white bread and as inviting as a frigid snow-covered field in the middle of Montana. Her cheap blinds are rarely open, which means the room is always too dark. There is a bed with metal handrails that are able to rise from each side. Next to the single bed is a small nightstand with a clock that I always set to digital time, but it refuses to stay in sync.

The state pays for the room because my grandmother ran out of money back during Obama's first term. Although, if you were to ask her—and her name is Eloise Dickens—what money is, she'd probably just blink at you. And maybe smile, but that would depend on your tone.

Every time I walk in, I shake my head and pull open the blinds. "Don't you want to see something, Grandma?"

I love describing the sky to her. It's like a painting to me, and like any artwork, the possibilities of describing it are endless. And although I could never paint anything as amazing, I like to try describing what I see as if I'm the artist.

"Hmmm." I ponder thoughtfully. "I'm seeing turbulent clouds on a rocky sea of blues." I pretty much just make things up, while trying to sound artistic and maybe somewhat pompous. Nobody but me is listening anyway.

My grandma almost always sits in her faded pink recliner. Normally she's watching *The Doctors* when I arrive after school. *The Doctors* is this lame "medical" show, but really it's just entertainment with all these attractive-looking people giving "medical" advice. Though, I also use the term "watching" loosely. My grandmother has no idea what is being said on that show. But her real doctor, at the nursing home—his name is Dr. Book—says that she likes the noise. I honestly don't know how he knows that, because I doubt my grandmother has ever said, "I like the TV on for the noise." Especially because my grandmother doesn't really have cogent thoughts anymore. But I don't question the doctor.

The clock is out of sync, even though I adjusted it yesterday. I go over and adjust it back two minutes. "No speeding up time," I joke.

My grandmother just smiles. Her curly white hair rests tightly against her scalp.

I sit on her perfectly made bed, which she doesn't make. "So, did you see that white light last night?"

"Light?" she asks.

"Yes. Around midnight. Did you see it?"

The nursing home that my grandmother stays in is

only about five blocks from my house. My house, for reference, sits on the eastern edge of town. And Whitehall is a town. A town of maybe three thousand people. I figure the light would have been just as bright here.

"Yes," my grandma says, "I'd like some."

"No." I shake my head. "Last night, Grandma. Did you see a bright light come from your window?" I point at the window, not sure if that helps or not.

She smiles and nods. "Nice window."

I let out a small sigh, but I don't get mad. I knew I wasn't going to get any useful information from her. But I had to try. My grandma has been known to surprise me with lucid moments, and sometimes even a lucid day. But those haven't happened for at least a year now, and Dr. Book doesn't think they will anymore. Isn't it kind of sad to think that you'll never think clearly again? But I guess it's only sad if you can think about it.

The new nurse, Susan McLean, walks into the room. "Oh, hi, Charlie." Every time Ms. McLean sees me, her face lights up as if I were some long-lost child of hers. Even though she started working here only a few weeks ago, and even though our conversations are limited, she is already one of my favorite people.

"Hi, Ms. McLean." She insisted I call her Susan when I first met her, but I don't want to be so casual with the woman who takes care of my grandma.

"Call me Susan, Charlie." She bends down in front of my grandma. "Hi, Eloise. Having a good afternoon? Your grandson is here to see you again."

"Grandson?" asks my grandma.

I stand in the corner of the room watching, waiting for

Ms. McLean—Susan—to finish her work. I like to stay out of her way.

Ms. McLean points to me. "You remember Charlie?"

My grandma looks at me absently and smiles just as absently. "Is he home from work already? I haven't had time to make dinner."

Ms. McLean looks at me and smiles ruefully, then turns back to my grandma. "I'm here to take your vitals, okay?" The state must not know that this particular nursing home exists, because everything is so old and worn—including the nursing equipment. Ms. McLean checks my grandma's heart rate, then checks her forehead for any temperature, which is easier than trying to get my grandma to keep a thermometer in her mouth. Finally Ms. McLean checks her blood pressure.

Watching Ms. McLean work, I wonder why everything in my life seems so abandoned and unloved—from my grandma's nursing home, to my high school, to my house, to this town in general.

Okay, so I'm being melodramatic. But really, who pays attention to forgotten people in forgotten towns? Or maybe it's just me who wants to forget about it all?

# THE LOST ABYSS

●●●●●

Night has descended. I stare out the window in my bedroom and then wonder if the website has been updated yet. Near the window is a small wooden desk that I inherited from my mother after she disappeared. She used it to handwrite long, meandering manifestos on contemporary society, and I use it to hold my ancient laptop. I click on the Montana UFO Sightings website. I go to the Sightings page, which still hasn't been updated. Could I have been the only person to have heard and seen what I heard and saw?

I swear I'm not making it up.

I click on the Contact page. This will be the first time I've ever written to Meridian X. That's all it says for her name—no last name or anything, other than *X*.

I ask if anyone spotted anything in Whitehall, Montana, yesterday around midnight. I tell her what I heard and saw and that I am looking for confirmation. Maybe someone else saw the same light? Heard the same noise? I click send.

After a few seconds of waiting, staring at my inbox, I close my laptop. I go back to the window and stare out into the Great Beyond, but all I see is darkness tonight.

"Where are you?" I ask under my breath.

A Great Nothingness echoes back to me.

# NO HABLO INGLÉS

· · · · ·

Ms. Monakey's Spanish classroom is overly decorated. There are probably no fewer than fifty posters hanging up, and they cover every square inch of formerly bare wall. Each poster has a Spanish word and a drawing accompanying it. For instance, there's "*manzana*" and a drawing of a red apple. Or "*chica*" and a little Dora the Explorer–type cartoon girl waving. I guess Ms. Monakey doesn't want us to forget some of the more common Spanish words, but the posters do seem a little childish.

Ms. Monakey is a nice teacher, but she is a redheaded girl with pale skin and freckles. So I'm occasionally caught off guard when she speaks Spanish. But I guess Whitehall, Montana, gets Irish-looking girls to teach Spanish. We're probably lucky to even have a Spanish class.

Sitting at my desk, waiting for first period to start, I check my email, and there's nothing from Meridian X. So I pull up the Montana UFO Sightings website to see if anything has been updated there, but there's still nothing. This is frustrating because that site is supposed to be an authority on all things paranormal in the state, but it hasn't been updated in more than a month.

"Same site?" comes a familiar voice. "Or should I still mind my own business?"

Seth stands over me. "Oh. Uh." I hit the home button on my phone, and the site disappears.

"What are you looking for?" he asks.

"Just seeing if they had any information on that bright light from the other night."

"Ah," says Seth, taking his seat behind me. "Do they?"

"No."

"So you believe in UFOs, then?"

I chuckle like he's crazy. "Not really. Do you?"

He smiles and pulls off the camera from around his neck. "Not sure. Never seen one. But maybe they're out there in the Great Beyond." He uses his hand to gesture through the air as if covering everything.

I nod. But deep inside I am all butterflies because he also uses the phrase "the Great Beyond." "Maybe," I say back. "I like your camera. Do you work for the school newspaper or something?"

"Nah," he says. "I just love photography. And you never know when an opportunity for a great shot will present itself."

Students finish filing into class as the final bell rings, and Ms. Monakey stands, clasps her hands, and says, "Okay, class. Let's begin."

As she speaks Spanish, my mind drifts.

About halfway through class I hear an ear-rattling buzz before a white light blinds the room. The light fades quickly, like a camera flash. The same light I saw in my bedroom.

Ms. Monakey's wide eyes search everywhere. "What's going on?" Students are looking around quizzically. But I know what's happening, so I sit confidently. Quietly. My hands are folded as if waiting for my name to be called.

The classroom door bursts open, with smoke hurling through the classroom. As the smoke clears, three aliens about six feet tall walk in. They have big rounded triangle-shaped heads and super skinny bodies. Their eyes are like a fly's (big, multiple lenses) and they have one slit about an inch long for their noses. Their skin is green—no, gray. They quickly scan the room from the doorway, and the screaming students stop.

"You," says the alien in front of the pack. "Charlie. Come with us. We're here to release you from Spanish class and from this miserable existence you call a life."

The students cheer for me as I rise from my desk. Seth high-fives me, and Ms. Monakey mouths "Nice work," then winks at me.

"Charlie? Earth to Charlie."

I snap back to class as Ms. Monakey waves her hand at me to get my attention. The class snickers.

"Sorry."

"Where did you go, Charlie? You looked like you were in some other world." She shakes her head and says, "Please pay attention. I asked, what is the word for 'apple' in Spanish?"

Damn, where is that poster? I scan the wall. . . .

I hear a whisper behind me. *"Manzana."*

I repeat the word, more loudly.

Ms. Monakey looks at me. "Good. Next time try it without Seth's help."

The bell rings, and I turn to Seth. "Thanks for helping me."

He shrugs as he puts his camera back around his neck. "Easy one." He grabs his backpack. "Hey, Charlie. Where do you eat lunch?"

I'm not sure I heard him clearly. No one has ever asked me that. I blink. "Uh?"

Seth laughs. "That thing between fourth and fifth period, when you fill your stomach with nutrients or pizza?"

"Oh, right. That. I don't usually. I mean, I eat. But I usually go to . . ." I realize that I don't want to tell him where I eat lunch because I don't want him to think I'm a loser. "Why do you want to know?" I eye him suspiciously.

"I just haven't seen you in the cafeteria. I'd like to eat lunch with you."

"Uh-huh," I say slowly.

He chuckles. "Don't be so suspicious. I swear, I will not throw food at you."

"Okay. That's one possibility. What about stuffing food down my pants? Squashing it on my head? Or—"

"Jesus, what kind of person do you take me for?"

We make our way out of Ms. Monakey's classroom and into the hallway. As we walk, I say, "You know that talking to me is social suicide, right? You're aware of that? I don't even want to imagine what would happen if you were seen eating lunch with me. Take my advice, Seth. Stay far away." I feel so stupid. Why am I saying these things? Why can't I just be happy that someone wants to eat lunch with me?

Seth gazes between people in the hallway. "Well, you seem to be more interesting than most around here."

"An amoeba is more interesting than most around here. That doesn't say too much."

I freeze in my tracks. Seth stops quickly too. "What?" he asks.

Walking toward us is Jennifer Bennett(!), the school's hottest girl. She is a sophomore and is news editor for the school newspaper, until next year, when she becomes managing editor. I realize that I stopped walking, so I get my feet moving again, except that they're not moving.

Oh shit. Here she comes.

"Just act natural," I tell him, thinking that everyone acts as weirdly as I do around Jennifer Bennett.

"Are you going to fill me in?"

Yes, I want to fill him in, but what's to say when she's so close and I can't get my feet to move? "That's Jennifer Bennett."

"Yeah. I have a few classes with her. So?" says Seth. I think he was expecting more to that story.

"She's—"

Seth looks at me. "You like her?"

My face burns. Okay, so there are a couple of reasons why I like her. It's not just because I find her physically attractive. She's smart. She's caring. And she has stood up for me in the past. In fact, she was the only one who didn't make fun of me after the town heard about what my mom did.

She's right next to us, and I turn away from her so that she can't see me. Not the best strategy for winning a girl over. But I haven't fully thought through my strategy of how to get her to like me, and being stuck to the middle of a school hallway doesn't say much in the way of confidence.

My head turns quickly back to her when I hear Seth

say, "Hey, Jennifer." He says it so casually, like it's not tearing him up to speak to her.

Jennifer smiles. "Seth, right?"

I'm not sure I even comprehend what's happening.

"Nice camera," she continues. "We're looking for someone to take some pictures for the newspaper next year. Interested?"

"Absolutely."

"Awesome. Stop by the newspaper room after school. I'll get you a form."

Jennifer Bennett(!) is having a conversation a foot away from me. Though, she doesn't even acknowledge my presence. Then again, I am trying to pretend I'm a fake plant. Something that blends into its surroundings. I'm apparently succeeding.

Seth turns. "And you know Charlie."

Suddenly Jennifer Bennett's eyes are drilling holes into my soul.

After she leaves, I realize that she might've said something. I might've said something. Or maybe nobody said anything. How awkward would that have been? All I know is that once she's gone, Seth turns to me and says, "She seems nice. Why don't you talk to her?"

I gulp. My brain slowly returns to a functioning level.

Seth laughs and shakes his head. "See you in the cafeteria, Charlie."

Hearing the donkey sounds of the Ass Trio down the hall, I will my feet to move before I'm seen. Though, I still largely feel like a fake plant.

# SO THIS IS WHAT THE CAFETERIA SMELLS LIKE

•••••

I'm sitting in World Cultures watching the clock tick from 11:58 to 11:59 as my thumbs fidget. Lunch is in one minute. I typically avoid places like the cafeteria, where large groups of students gather without prominent adult supervision. So naturally I'm nervous about eating lunch with Seth in the cafeteria.

My heart flutters when the lunch bell rings and people hastily make their way out of the classroom. I want my feet to grow roots and stay planted here. But instead I inch my way down the brown-tiled hallway with my sack lunch (that I pack every day so that I can eat anywhere but the cafeteria).

Our school lunch situation is a bit different from most, at least from what I've been told. Whitehall High School students—even the supremely popular ones—eat in the cafeteria. It is for one simple reason: pizza. Our pizza place in town has about three tables and is the slowest pizza place in the world. And if you're thinking about

McDonald's or Taco Bell, well, I'm sad to report that Whitehall is too small to have those. We have one Subway, which is connected to the gas station near the interstate. That's the same place that I work at—but I work on the other side of the gas station, at the diner. So most of the students eat in the cafeteria.

I hesitate near the double doors as I hear the chaos of sounds coming from inside. Once I turn the corner, all bets are off on what happens next. For all I know, everyone's ready to throw food at me.

At the beginning of the school year, I came to eat in the cafeteria before I knew better. Live and learn, right? I was alone. As usual. And I'd just gotten my pizza. I held my tray and looked around at all the familiar strangers, and slowly trudged to an empty table.

I felt awkward and self-conscious. I had just sat when I heard Joey's voice above me. "Hey, look. My favorite writer is here. And all by himself."

Matt and Psych stood next to him.

"Taking a break from your novel?"

I didn't look up at any of them. I took a bite of my pizza.

I felt Joey flick my ear as he laughed and said, "Come out of your study more often. I like you, DICK-ens. And you might make some friends."

My face turned beet red.

"That pizza looks good." He took it out of my hands and acted like he was going to take a bite but then dropped it onto the floor. "Whoops. Greasy."

All the students were laughing, and I felt exposed and

vulnerable. I felt like the entire school was against me. I just wanted to run away. That's all I ever want to do.

Joey leaned over the table and hugged me very exaggeratedly. "Love you, Charles." He laughed and flicked my ear again before walking off. Matt and Psych followed, but not without flicking my ear too.

After a few more not-so-pleasant encounters, I decided to forgo the cafeteria.

And eat alone.

I take a deep breath and face the cafeteria straight on. I scan the room and see that students are scattered from table to table, talking or eating or laughing. It's almost like no one is even aware of my existence at the cafeteria entrance—which is great.

I search but can't find Seth anywhere. I don't want to walk into the chaos that is the cafeteria, and it's small enough that I can see everyone anyway. If he's not here, then I guess I'll go back to my secret hiding place. I'm feeling duped, and as I turn, I bump right into him.

"Where you going, Charlie?"

"I thought you weren't coming."

"You thought I'd ditch you? Harsh. Mr. Roberts had to talk to me."

I need to shake off my insecurity. "Where do you want to sit?"

"I don't care. Lead the way."

I walk to the table that's closest to the doors. It's practically empty. "This is good. In case we have to make a run for it."

Seth laughs, because he thinks I'm joking.

Seth's talking as we eat our turkey sandwiches—I love turkey, but I'm transfixed by Jennifer Bennett sitting across the room. Her blond hair and slim face with her sharp nose and dark brown eyes make her so beautiful.

Seth clears his throat, and I look to him. He's staring at me, expectantly.

"Sorry?"

Seth laughs again. "Never mind. Nice glasses, by the way. I have contacts."

What is happening right now? Not only am I in the cafeteria, but someone cool is eating next to me and talking *to* me. And I can't get out of my head enough to enjoy it.

*Earth to Charlie. Come back.*

"So tell me something about yourself, besides the secret fact that you're into UFOs," Seth says.

I feel my face turn red. "You can't tell anyone that."

"My lips are sealed."

Then I wonder, why would Seth have my back? Why wouldn't he use this information to make my life hell and to gain some popularity?

"What are you thinking about now? It's like your brain is never quiet." Seth chuckles again as he takes a bite of his sandwich.

I watch him chew. "Are you a sophomore?"

Seth nods. "Yep."

This is just too weird. Why would a sophomore want to hang out with a freshman? Let alone me? This has to be a trap—and yet, it feels real.

"You know . . ." He stares at me as I talk. "I'm a freshman, right?" I'm ready for him to blink and grab his food and leave me right here. Not another word said. And you know what? I'd get it. I wouldn't even fault him for it.

So I'm bracing myself, but instead he laughs. "Yeah, I know. You're a freshman for a few more days and then you'll be a sophomore. Like me." He winks.

"Not sure it works like that," I say.

"Charlie, I don't care what grade you're in. It's not about that."

*Then what's it about?* I clear my throat. "So you're okay with it?"

Seth stares at me as he tries to figure out if I'm being serious. "Would I be sitting here eating lunch with you if I wasn't okay with it? Or if I didn't like you? Just, relax."

I nod, a heavy feeling in my chest. After so many years alone, I feel undeserving of a friend.

# THE THREE-LEGGED DOG AND HIS OBESE OWNER

·····

My next-door neighbor lives in a tiny, faded yellow house surrounded by a chain-link fence, with a narrow walkway leading up to three rust-color stained cement stairs. The yard is mostly dirt spots and rocks and weeds. My neighbor, Geoffrey, hasn't used his front door in probably a year or more. If he leaves his house, he uses the ramp in the back, which basically goes right to his car. Though, he stopped driving because, as he said, "I can't turn the wheel with my stomach in the way."

I knock at the front door, but then enter without waiting for Geoffrey. He told me a long time ago to just knock and enter. He said, "It'd take me eons to answer." As usual his house is pristine, the carpet always freshly vacuumed and everything dusted. He doesn't have piles of junk like one might think a shut-in would. Geoffrey once told me he hated pack rats and hoarders. He said that everything has its time and place, and people should realize that and not keep things after their use has finished. Not sure why

Geoffrey is so annoyed by other people's messes, but he is.

He sits on his new green love seat, which has a reinforced wooden base and doubles as his new bed. This is where I find him these days. Geoffrey outgrew his recliner around the time he outgrew his car. "Hi, Charlie." He coughs; his chins wobble.

He isn't watching TV like those fat stereotypes would like to have you believe. He has a laptop resting on his massive, quaking belly. He makes money as a freelance web designer. "Come, take a seat." Next to the love seat is the old recliner. "Do you want something to eat? Cookies? Or something to drink?"

I shake my head as I sit. "I'm okay."

Geoffrey whistles, which is followed by more coughing. I hear a jingle get louder and louder as Tickles runs into the front room and barks. He runs over to me, and I bend down and pet him. "Hi, Tickles."

The thing to know about Tickles is that he only has three legs. Well, three real legs. His fourth leg, which happens to be his front right, is prosthetic. It looks kind of like a single ski, but vertical, and the ski curves slightly out in front as it gets closer to the ground. It's a pretty awesome fake leg. I'm not entirely sure Tickles even knows he has a fake leg.

"Ready to go for a walk?" Geoffrey asks him.

Tickles barks and runs in a circle. Tickles is a small, brown curly-haired dog. He is a mutt that Geoffrey adopted from the Humane Society in Butte. This was back when Geoffrey could walk a dog.

Tickles is getting old, but he still needs his walks. So Geoffrey pays me twenty dollars a week to walk his dog.

Not that I do it for the money; I would definitely walk Tickles for free, but Geoffrey insists on paying.

With Tickles on the leash, I tell Geoffrey that I'll be back in a half hour. "See you soon, Charlie."

Because I live so close to the woods, I usually take Tickles along this dirt road into the forest. The road starts on the other side of my yard—near the trees. It's easy enough on Tickles's leg, but still out of Whitehall.

Our typical walks go something like this: Tickles always runs ahead of me and keeps that pace the entire way until we get to our turnaround spot. For an older dog with a fake leg, he is in remarkable health. He'll occasionally bark when he sees a bird, but otherwise he just keeps moving those little legs. After our turnaround spot, he moves more slowly and stays closer to me, with more frequent stops on the way back.

I inhale the fresh air as we begin today's walk. "Such a nice day out, Tickles." So I'm a person who talks to dogs. Don't judge; they're great listeners. Besides that, they never talk back or call you names.

I keep checking out the sky as we walk. "Tickles, did you know UFOs have been seen during the day almost as often as night? Kind of crazy, right? To think a UFO could be hiding in one of those foamy clouds."

Tickles stops to sniff the same tree he sniffs every time we pass. It's kind of scraggly, and that's probably on account of how many times it's been marked. "I have this romantic notion that it'll happen at night. Maybe it seems more plausible then. Like, at night our world opens up to let others in."

We're walking again, and I can't help but continue

looking up. Up to the sky. Up to the world above me.

"Tickles. Let's say you're an artist. How would you describe the sky?"

Tickles ignores me as he stares straight ahead, never really looking up. Never even acknowledging me. "Tickles!" I shout.

He yaps.

"No, that's a terrible description. Hmm." I put my finger to my chin. "This one is something I'll call *Haunted by the Unseen*, because maybe there's something behind those foamy clouds." I like using the word "foamy" to describe the clouds.

About a mile in, we stop at the usual log and rest. Then we turn around and head back. In typical fashion, Tickles slows his pace.

"Tickles, I can't help but notice that you always slow down on the way back. Is it because you're tired? Or because you don't want to go back home? Because if it's that, I get it. I bet your house is just as dreadful as mine." I quickly look at Tickles, feeling guilty. "I don't mean any disrespect toward Geoffrey. I just think that, given his limitations, you probably have to keep yourself entertained quite a bit, huh?"

Tickles doesn't even acknowledge my words or my existence as he trots by my side.

Geoffrey is in the same place I left him. After I unleash Tickles, he runs past Geoffrey and into the kitchen, bell ringing continuously.

"Good walk?" Geoffrey asks.

"You should come sometime."

Geoffrey laughs and then coughs. "That'd be the day."

I stand there. "Did you happen to hear a noise or see a bright light on Sunday night?"

Geoffrey studies my face. "Hmm. I don't think so."

"It was around midnight."

Geoffrey shrugs, and coughs. "I was sleeping. And I could sleep through an earthquake. So I don't recall anything. Why?"

"Just thought I heard something. And you live closest to me, so there was a good chance you heard it too."

"UFO, you think?"

Geoffrey is the only person in my life who takes me seriously with the UFO search. I mean, Seth might, but I haven't fully grasped his intentions. At least Geoffrey entertains that UFOs are real, that we humans aren't the only ones in the vastness of the universe.

I nod. UFO, I think.

# ROD'S DINER SURPRISE

• • • • •

I have no idea who Rod is or if there even is or ever was a Rod. But inside the Whitehall truck stop off Interstate 90 is Rod's Diner. Tonight's shift is about as busy as a typical night, which is to say a healthy mix of rushing around for a while and then having nothing to do, before rushing around again. I'm a busboy and have had the job for a couple of months; in Montana I can work limited hours at fourteen years old, and I'm almost fifteen, anyway. I only wanted the job because I'm almost allowed to get my learner's permit (I took the driver's ed course last fall), and I'm saving up for a truck. I'm ready to retire my bike.

It's about seven p.m., and I'm chatting with John, one of our regulars. John has a thick brown mustache with matching thick eyebrows, and he makes a weekly trip through Whitehall on his way to Spokane and back to Fargo. He is telling me about this time when he was driving and saw a Corvette flip right in front of him on some high mountain pass.

"Sos I hit the brakes hard, the tires just smokin' as they dug into the road. The back end of my truck swervin' like a fish out of water, almost pullin' me off the road and off the ledge." John takes a sip of his coffee. "Sos I get to a stop and jump out, running like a chicken with my head cut off at the car. One of the guys had been ejected right through the damn windshield. Sure as shit."

"Oh god. Did he live?"

John glares at me for interrupting. "And the other was trapped right there in his seat. The car was upside down, of course. Sos I'm yankin' on the door when—"

The door to Rod's Diner dings. I look over to see who is entering, out of habit mostly. But I actually recognize someone this time. Standing there is Ms. McLean— Susan—in her nursing scrubs, followed by . . . Seth?

I straighten up from the counter and say, "One sec, John." I probably look confused as I stare at Susan and Seth, trying to absorb the fact that they are related. Family? Mother and son? This makes total sense in retrospect. They both appeared at the same time: one in class, one at the nursing home. I just didn't put it together.

Susan spots me. "Charlie? What a surprise." Ms. McLean has an amazing ability to say everything so warmly, and again she has the largest smile.

Seth looks up from his phone. "Oh, hey, Charlie." He still has his camera hanging around his neck. Seth towers a good five inches above his mom. He also has on a flat-beaked baseball hat with some emblem on it. I don't recognize it, but it looks kind of like a Chinese letter to me. "I didn't know you worked here."

"I'm just the busboy, so you won't get free food out of me." Then in this weird German-sounding accent I say, "I don't have ze power."

I can be such an idiot sometimes.

I force a laugh to get me out of this awkward situation, and Susan follows. Seth just smiles.

I notice that Tammy is standing near us with two menus in her hands. "Oh, Tammy is ready to seat you."

Tammy smirks and mocks, "Are you sure ze show is over?" She chuckles. "I could use a few more laughs tonight. Especially because Billy split with me." She says that last part in a hushed voice. But she also says that last part at least once every month. Billy and her can never stay together for more than thirty consecutive days because it's against their relationship rules. Okay, that's a joke. Who knows why they can't stay together without splitting up and then getting back together. Tammy always says, "Someday I'm not going to take him back. That'll show him." But someday has not yet arrived. I'm not sure someday will ever arrive.

As Susan and Seth look over their menus, I try to make myself look busy. But every time I walk behind the counter, John asks, "Ready for the end of the story?"

I keep saying, "Sorry, John. Not yet." Then I pretend to work, hoping both Susan and Seth will notice all the moving and hustling I'm doing. For some reason I just don't want them to see me standing around talking.

On my way to the far side of the restaurant with a broom, Seth says, "Hey, Charlie." He waves me over and then points at one of the items on the menu. "What is Rod's Diner Surprise? And is it supposed to say 'diner' or 'dinner'? Because wouldn't 'dinner' make more sense? Unless it's like a breakfast thing."

"Uh. I think it varies from day to day." Not sure why I said "I think," because it does vary from day to day. That's why it's called a surprise.

"Do you know what it is today?" he asks.

"Some kind of stew. Not sure, though. I think Tammy knows. But to be honest, I'd stick with eggs or sandwiches. Everything else here is kind of nasty."

"So that's a no to the lasagna," says Susan, smiling.

I shrug. "Some people like it."

"I'm kidding, Charlie."

"Oh. Yeah." I laugh. God, I am feeling so awkward in front of both of them, like I'm not good enough to even be around. So I try to take the attention off me. "So you're related?"

"You don't see our striking resemblance?" asks Seth sarcastically.

"Seth mostly takes after his father, but he has my eyes and chin and hair," says Susan.

"Oh, will your dad be joining you for dinner tonight?"

"He would if he wasn't in prison," says Seth.

"Seth!" says Susan.

My face feels like it's on fire. "Oh. I'm sorry for asking."

Seth shakes his head. "I'm kidding, Charlie. He lives in Seattle."

Gulp. "Oh."

Tammy comes up behind me. "Ready to order?"

Susan says, "Yes, I think so."

I bow away. "Talk to you later," I say to no one in particular.

A little while later John stands and says, "I guess you'll have to hear the ending next time. I'm back to the road."

"Next time. Of course!" I feel like a jerk for brushing him off. But I'm too nervous with Susan and Seth in the restaurant. I feel like I have to impress them.

Their plates cleaned of food and their bill paid, Ms. McLean and Seth stand to leave. He shouts across the mostly empty diner, "I'll see you first thing tomorrow in *Español*, Charlie." He has so much confidence. And enthusiasm. I could never shout across a restaurant like that—even if there were only a couple of other people around.

I don't know what to say. "Sure." Which is a ridiculous response, so I add, "Of course."

He winks at me.

Then I say, "Sounds great."

*Give it a rest, Charlie.*

I finish sweeping the diner and do my end-of-shift cleaning duties. When I finish cleaning, I'm allowed to go home. It's dark, but I still ride my bike.

# NO KISS GOOD NIGHT

.....

When I open the front door and look into the living room, I find my dad watching TV on the new flat-screen he purchased. Never mind that the washing machine sucks or that the lawn mower hasn't worked right in years. He saved up for a larger TV to replace a perfectly functioning one. I guess that really only bothers me because I am the one who has to deal with the laundry and the yard.

There are five empty beer cans on the coffee table next to his recliner. The living room is dark except for the blue light coming from the TV, which only slightly illuminates my dad. The light makes his vacant, glossy eyes and rigid body appear zombielike. He has been drinking more ever since my mom disappeared. I think he's mad that the aliens wanted her more than he did.

"Hi, Dad," I say as I enter the living room.

Without diverting his eyes away from the TV, he says, "You smell." He's referring to the grease smell that usually accompanies me home from a shift at Rod's.

The funny thing is that my dad always smells like alcohol when he gets home. Really, I should be the one telling him that he smells. But I keep my mouth shut—always the safest bet, I've found, with anything. Keeping my mouth shut has been how I've managed to get this far.

"How was work?" he asks.

"Fine." I say good night and trudge up the narrow stairway to the bathroom to shower.

After my shower, I'm tired, but I have to stand in front of my bedroom window and stare out into the Great Beyond. I don't want to miss another opportunity. The aliens have to be coming back soon, right? And why not tonight?

But I grow tired of standing after twenty minutes, so I crawl into bed. I'm comforted by knowing that if a UFO arrives, it'll wake me up with the loud noise and bright light. Right?

The world outside stays dark, and with my lamp now turned off, my room quickly settles back into its tomb-like feeling.

# THE ASS TRIO STRIKES AGAIN

·····

My alarm beeps, and I wonder how many times I can hit snooze without being incredibly late to school. I have to keep telling myself, *Only two more school days left before summer. Only two more.* But then I wonder if I'll see Seth during the summer. The thought of not seeing Seth for the summer depresses me.

Before I get out of bed, I put on my glasses and check my email to see if Meridian has responded. When I click on my mail icon, a new email downloads, and it's from her!

> Hello, Charlie,
> No one has reported anything to me—
> and I didn't see anything on this side
> of the divide! You're the first I've heard
> from on this. So thank you for informing
> me! I will update the website tonight
> with your details. And credit you with
> the sighting. Do you want just your first

name, or first and last? Let me know.
Best,
Meridian X
P.S. I wonder what they were doing over
there???

I put my phone down and feel a sense of abandonment
from her email. I should be elated at getting credit, but I
wasn't writing her to report it. I was writing to confirm it,
and now I am left no closer to the truth. I lie in bed thinking about how quickly she believes a random email, until
I gaze at the clock, and bolt up.

I'm running later than normal, so I'm pedaling as fast as
possible. (See: why I'm working at Rod's.) Usually I like to
get to class before the school is teeming with idiots.

But this morning I'm not so lucky. I lock my bike
and notice that the Ass Trio, plus a few other people, are
standing in a group on the sidewalk between the parking lot and school. It would be better to walk all the way
around the school than to walk in their general vicinity,
but I am already running late, and I want to talk to Seth
before class starts. Besides, I figure Joey and his group
are all talking and involved in each other's business. Why
would they notice me? I'll put my head down and walk
quickly around them, and they'll never see me.

They see me.

Matt says, "Hey, Joe. Look at DICK-ens."

Psych chortles.

My head is still down at this point; I'm trying to ignore
them. I stupidly think that if I don't acknowledge them,

then maybe they will leave me alone. It hasn't worked yet.

Joey laughs. "Charles Dickens. Hey, Charles! Come here."

Staring straight down at the cracks in the sidewalk, I mumble under my breath, "It's 'Charlie,' you ass."

"Watch out!" someone yells.

My head snaps up as a paper cup comes flying right at me. I duck out of the way, but what appears to be Coke lands on my left leg and splatters up to my shorts and the lower part of my shirt. Not to mention that it makes my bare leg sticky and my sock wet.

I shake my head. I hear the asses laugh.

Only two more days. Two more days.

I hurry into the building and dart into the bathroom just as the five-minute warning bell rings.

I turn on the faucet and wait for the warm water to come.

*Come on. Come on.*

The one-minute warning bell rings, and my shorts hang on me, drenched in water. I hesitate, wondering whether it would be better to show up to class late and dry, or wet and on time.

I figure the "wet and on time" is the best decision because everyone probably already knows what happened anyway. I might as well not get a tardy detention on my last week of school.

There is giggling and some pointing as my left shoe squeaks, and my sock feels squishy as I walk across the room to my seat, but I ignore everyone. Except Seth, who cocks his head at me. "What happened to you?"

"I don't want to talk about it," I say after sitting down.

The final bell rings.

He pokes my back. "Seriously. What happened?"

I shake my head. "Just a mishap getting to school. Forget about it."

Ms. Monakey stands in front of the room and clasps her hands. "All right, class. Let's begin."

Seth pokes me in the back again.

"What?" I sharply whisper in annoyance.

"Why can't you tell me?" he asks quietly.

I shake my head. I'm also pissed that I couldn't talk to Seth before class.

He whispers, "Tell me at lunch?"

I didn't realize he wanted to have lunch with me again. That makes the morning more palatable. "Okay."

# THE SMELL OF ROT NEVER CHANGES

•••••

I can't believe I am having lunch in the cafeteria for the second day in a row. It still stinks in here.

Seth sits next to me and takes huge bites of his pizza. I adjust my glasses and loudly unwrap my sandwich. "Let me guess. Turkey?"

I nod.

"Why is it wrapped in tinfoil?" Seth asks.

"We're out of plastic wrap."

Seth wipes his mouth with the back of his hand. "So are you going to tell me what happened?"

"It's over. No big deal."

"Then tell me."

I sigh. "Someone threw Coke at me."

"No way," says Seth. He seems genuinely shocked, which shocks me. "Asshole. Who was it?"

"Doesn't matter." But Seth doesn't stop staring at me until I say the name. "Joey Richards."

"I know who he is." Seth takes his last bite of pizza.

"Let's plan our revenge on Joey Richards."

"No way. It's over. Let's move on."

"Fine. If that's what you want." I notice that Seth keeps his eye on Joey across the cafeteria for a second longer.

Seth's being protective of me, which makes me feel respected. It fills me with warmth. I'm now thinking of summer and how quickly it'll be here and how I don't want to have Seth out of my life, which is a weird thought when I've really only known him for a couple of days.

The bell rings, and we both get up to leave. "I'll talk to you later, Charlie." Seth heads to the door but then stops, forcing people to walk around him. "Oh. I almost forgot." He hands me a torn piece of paper from his pocket. "Text me sometime." He disappears with the rest of the students.

I stand there clutching his number in my hand.

# THE SHEETS GUY

· · · · ·

As I walk down the hallway of the nursing home to my grandmother's room after school, Susan spots me. "She didn't have a good night last night. She had an accident in bed, and if it happens again, she'll have to start wearing Depends. At least to bed."

"Depends?"

"Adult diapers."

When I get to my grandma's darkened room, I pull the blinds up. "Hi, Grandma." She is sitting in her recliner, thumbs fidgeting with each other. "Have some light."

"Are you here to change my bed?"

"No, Grandma. It's me." I point to my chest. "Charlie."

"The sheets guy?"

I shake my head. "Your grandson." Her bed has already been made.

"Charlie?" says Grandma. The way she says my name makes it seem like she has no idea who I am.

I reach for her clock and adjust it back two minutes. I

set the clock back on the nightstand. I sit on her bed, and we stare at each other. "What do you want to do today?"

"Charlie?" my grandma says again. But it's as if she's a parrot echoing without any sort of emotion.

"Let's go for a walk. It's nice outside." That's one thing Dr. Book said to me last week: get her up and moving more. The nursing home staff tries, and sometimes with success, but she seems more interested in keeping the recliner warm all day. Dr. Book said she'll deteriorate a lot quicker without exercise.

She knows what I'm talking about when I say "walk" and turns her head away from me.

"Come on, Grandma. You used to love to go for walks. I'll go with you."

"Charlie?"

"Yes, Grandma." I put my hands out for her to grab hold.

"Where's Harold?"

"Come on, take my hands." I can't keep answering that question, which started coming up a few months ago. I don't like to repeatedly tell my grandma that her husband died. Why couldn't she just remember that? Of all the things to forget. It's like she keeps reliving the shocking news of his death every time I tell her. I don't like continually breaking her heart.

I'm so relieved when Grandma puts her hands into mine. I'm pulling her up when I hear a *click*.

I turn to see Seth at the door with his camera up to his eye, aimed right at my grandma and me. "I hope you don't mind, but that was a beautiful moment," he says, lowering the camera.

I think I do mind, but I don't really know why. "Are you stalking me?" I ask jokingly.

"Harold?" asks Grandma, turning to the door.

"No, Grandma. Seth," I say.

"Charlie?"

I sigh. "I'm Charlie." I manage to get Grandma up. I turn to Seth. "We're going for a walk."

"Want company?" he asks.

"If you want. But you may go crazy."

"Too late," says Seth. He smiles at me.

I'm holding her up, and I turn to her. "Let's go, Grandma." But she just stands there. Defiant.

"What can I do?" Seth asks, coming forward.

"Can you grab her walker? It's in the corner by the window."

Seth unfolds it and places it in front of her. She knocks it over with her free arm.

"Grandma," I say, picking it up. "You like outside." I look to Seth. "I think she'd prefer to sit on the recliner forever."

"Grandmas," says Seth.

She tips the walker over again.

"Maybe we should get her a wheelchair?" asks Seth.

"Wouldn't that defeat the purpose of the walk?" I ask.

"Fresh air?"

"No, exercise."

We finally shuffle out of the room and into the hallway. I think it's sad how my grandma lives in the nursing home and none of the other residents even seem to acknowledge her or know who she is. Strangers under the same roof.

"A miracle!" I say when we exit the building. "We actually made it outside."

Seth takes a picture of me holding my grandma's arm as we walk down the sidewalk. We abandoned the idea of the walker when she wouldn't leave it in front of her for more than twelve seconds without knocking it over.

The walk is slow going, with Grandma taking small shuffling steps along the sidewalk. Though, she seems happy or at least content to be shuffling.

"Your grandma's awesome," Seth says.

She doesn't even react to us talking about her. She just keeps shuffling.

"Used to be so much more awesome," I say. But I hate myself after saying that, as if she's somehow worth less now.

The sun is shining brightly, but I notice clouds building to the west. "How would you describe the sky?"

Seth narrows his eyes as he looks up. "The sky?"

"Yeah, like if it's a painting, what would you say? How would you describe it?"

"I'm a photographer. I get to describe the sky through pictures." Seth stops walking, aims the camera up, and steadies his hand as he snaps a picture. I keep moving with Grandma. I don't want to stop her progress now that she's moving. Besides, I have to get ready for work soon.

# EXTREME CONDITIONS

•••••

Whitehall is on the east side of the Continental Divide, and most of the storms get trapped on the west side of the mountains. We rarely have storms in Whitehall because of our location. Usually any clouds roll on by, but some of the storms we get can be pretty fierce.

I'm at Rod's Diner, cleaning tables and watching the dark clouds roll in. I just hope, since I have to bike home, that the storm is over by the time my shift is done. But these clouds look mean.

Larry is the manager of Rod's, and he happens to be working tonight. I hate when Larry works, because he is a royal dick. Larry comes up to me as I'm washing off a table and says, "My deaf and dumb grandma moves faster."

I want to say, "Then why isn't she the manager?" But I keep quiet, and he moves on.

It's a bit pathetic, but I keep looking at the door—even when the bell doesn't ring—to see if Seth and Susan are standing there. I know it wouldn't make sense for them to show up two nights in a row, but I can at least hope.

The clouds have completely taken over our little town, and it's quite dark out, and as I'm watching the door, thinking about Seth and Susan, I hear thunder and the rain start to pour.

During my "lunch break," which is after most people finish dinner, I head into the convenience store on the other side of the building to kill some time.

At the back of the store, there's a small rack with books and magazines. I am browsing when a book catches my eye: *Montana UFO Sightings*. I knew there was a book, written by Meridian X, because there is a big clunky section on her website talking about it. The book has been out for about six months, but I never in a million years thought I'd see it at the convenience store in Whitehall, Montana.

I look around to see if anybody is paying attention to me. The coast is clear, so I pick up the book, with its slick green cover and a picture of a gray-and-white school yard with a black saucerlike object in the far right corner. The saucer does look like a UFO, but I am as skeptical as most. I know that the odds of seeing aliens and UFOs are minimal at best and that most people just make these things up. But I have to believe. It's kind of a matter of life and death.

I want to buy the book, but I don't have fifteen dollars on me. So I put it back.

When I get back from my lunch break, Rod's Lame Diner is still empty. Larry walks right up to me, his cocky attitude in tow. "Listen, it's slow. I'm going to let you go early tonight."

I look out the window, and the sheets of rain show no sign of slowing. A river gushes from the rainspouts and down the asphalt to the road. "Uh. Okay."

I head to the back hallway, which connects the break room, freezer, and kitchen together. After I clock out, I turn and see Tammy next to me. "I'm done with him, Charlie. He's screwed up one too many times."

I already know she's talking about her boyfriend, Billy. Again.

"What did he do?" I want to add "this time," but I stop myself.

"Last night he came home late. Like, three a.m. And I was like, 'Where have you been?' And he's like, 'The bar.' And so I say, 'Bars close at two. Where've you been for the last hour, huh?' And he's all like, 'I walked around town.' And I'm like, 'Like hell you did.' And he's like, 'I just needed some time to think.' So I stormed to my bedroom and locked him out. He knocked on the door for a while and then just fell asleep on the couch. Dumb buffoon.

"My girlfriends say I need to dump his butt for good." I wait to see if she'll continue, but she just rubs her temples. "I better get back to work. I hear my few tips decreasing by the second." She hustles back out to the dining room before I even have a chance to say anything.

I don't see the rain lightening up anytime soon, so I head into the diner and take a seat at the table closest to the front door. The hostess sign half-blocks the table.

It takes Larry a few minutes to spot me, but he storms over. "Tables for customers only."

"Are you serious? I work here."

"Are you buying something?"

I stare at him, slightly dumbfounded that he's really this anal about things.

"Customers only," he repeats, and walks away.

There are three customers in the entire restaurant.

I go outside and stand under the gas pump awning. The pounding of the rain on the metal is deafening. I am stuck for as long as the storm rages on. It could be another five minutes or two hours.

I remember that I have Seth's number but I have yet to text him my number. So I pull out my phone. Hey. This is Charlie.

After a few seconds: Hey, Charlie.

I look at his words and wonder what to say. I think about putting my phone away, but then I type: Now you have my number. I debate on adding a smiley face but think that's probably too much emotion for the situation.

Feeling stupid after pressing send (he clearly knows he has my number now), I put my phone away. My phone vibrates, and I smile because he responded to my dumb text.

Glad to have it. What took you so long???

I smile like a dork, and my heart flutters. That text definitely caught me off guard. He hasn't turned on me yet.

Sorry. Was at work. Stuck here until the storm lets up.

My phone stops vibrating.

Large puddles are forming, and the sides of the roads are small streams. I can't believe the strength of this storm. I just want this to be over so I can get home.

A Toyota 4Runner pulls up next to me, and Seth sticks his head out the window. "Need a ride?" He grins.

"What are you doing?"

"Get in."

"Really?"

Seth nods. "Really."

"Oh, I have my bike."

"Go get it. We'll put it in back."

I notice the smell of the car as I slide into the passenger seat. Seth's car smells lemony in a distinct, artificial plastic sort of way. I wipe the water off my glasses.

"I didn't know you drove. Or had a car."

"I have my learner's permit." Seth grins. "And this is my mom's car."

Seth shifts into gear and then pulls onto the road that heads toward the main street. The only real street in town.

"If you have a learner's permit, you can only drive if you're with someone over eighteen," I say.

Seth turns and grins at me again. He shrugs.

I'm freaked out that we'll get into a car crash, but I'm also glad that I no longer have to wait for the storm to end.

He clears his throat, and he's looking at me. "You're welcome."

"Oh. Thanks."

"What are friends for?"

Friends. That's a word I haven't heard in years. It feels strange as I turn it over and over in my mind. I want to smile, but instead I tell him to watch the road, because he's smiling at me.

I give Seth directions to my house, his wipers going a hundred miles a minute.

"Do you like working at that diner?"

"It's not that bad. The manager is a jerk. But everyone else is cool."

Seth nods. "My mom wants me to get a job this

summer, but I'd rather spend my time taking pictures. I keep telling her that taking pictures will help me prepare for my future more. Don't you get sick of that saying?"

"What saying?"

"'Prepare for your future.'" The sound of the rain and the flip-flap of the windshield wipers are hard to ignore. "I hate that. Adults are always saying it."

"Well, I'm only really working because I'm saving up for a truck. And then I won't be stuck at work when it rains."

"But then I won't have the chance to pick you up."

When he pulls up to my house, I notice how old, empty, and quiet it looks. My dad isn't home yet from the bar.

I don't want to go inside. I want to ask if Seth wants to hang out, but I also don't want him to laugh at me or say no. But then I realize that he picked me up (illegally) without being asked, and he did kind of just throw out the 'friend' word, so maybe I have a chance.

"What are you doing tonight?" I ask.

"Not homework."

"Want to . . . I don't know. Hang out?"

He smiles. "Thought you'd never ask."

"Your house?"

"Not yours? We're already here."

"No. . . . It's . . . too messy."

Seth stares at me a little longer before putting the car into gear and driving off, spraying a large fan of water from his tires. He swerves a bit, and I curse under my breath in fright. He just laughs.

# A COOKIE-FILLED STORY

.....

Seth's house is unlike mine in almost every way. To compare our houses would be to compare Candy Land to a graveyard. Or something. After entering his room, it becomes very apparent that Seth isn't from Whitehall. "Wow. Your room is awesome." He owns a large Mac monitor and a comforter with the skyline of New York City.

Plus, about twelve pictures hang in clusters of three or four all over the walls.

I'm looking back at the black-and-white skyline comforter. "Have you been to New York?"

Seth shakes his head. "No. But I want to go to college there."

"For what?" I ask, sitting on his bed.

"Photography."

"Duh," I say, slapping my forehead.

Seth plops down next to me on his bed. "I love big cities."

"That's a really sweet computer."

"I have it for my pictures. I can see them better to edit."

I look over and see a large flat-screen TV hanging on his wall in line with his bed. "How big is that?"

"Forty-two inches."

"That's huge."

Seth laughs. "I'll have to see your room sometime."

"Ah, no. That'll never happen now."

"Oh, come on."

"Nuh-uh. You have so much cool stuff. I look like Oliver Twist compared to you." I immediately regret that choice of comparison.

"Is your name the only reason why you're made fun of?" He moves again, to rest against his headboard with his hands behind his head.

I feel uncomfortable with that question, to be honest. I have never had to talk about why I am a constant target. Everyone just knows, and I'm not sure I want Seth to know all my faults, or my family's. But I get the sense that his intentions are genuine.

"There are a lot of reasons I'm teased. But it started in elementary school." I stand up and look at a black-and-white photograph on his wall. There are two small mountains that slope to a flat horizon in the middle of the picture, where the sun is setting. The mountains, the ground, all look barren. And the sun is only showing a sliver above the horizon. "Did you take this?"

"I took all the pictures in here."

I look at another black-and-white one. It's a face of an old man, and really close up, so you can see all the wrinkles and his big, black-framed glasses. He has wisps of gray hair falling around his ears, but he's bald on top. He's not smiling but not frowning either.

Another picture is a small aluminum boat on a mountain lake surrounded by trees. There's one lone fisherman with one lone pole hanging out of the boat. But the boat is far away, so you can't really make out any details.

"You're really good."

"Thanks." He smiles.

Seth is waiting for me to continue my story. I guess I can tell him a few reasons why I'm teased, but I won't tell him about my mother. At least not yet. And anyway, he will probably hear about it sooner or later. I mean, it's like one of the town's best stories. I doubt it will ever die. So I decide to tell him about the easy stuff: "Let's just say I'm a walking cliché."

Seth's eyes narrow. "How so?"

"Gym class. Fumble. Fumble. Fumble."

"Well, not everyone's athletic."

"You look like you're pretty athletic."

"I do okay at a few things. Track is my favorite."

I shake my head. "I can run, but I can't catch anything. Half the time I was called a girl in grade school."

"Kids can be mean."

"Once a target, always a target. I don't even think it's personal anymore." I turn to stare at the sunset picture again. "I mean, I guess it is. But I have to tell myself it's not. Otherwise, not sure I could make it through."

There is a knock on Seth's door. "Yeah?"

"Cookies," says Ms. McLean on the other side of the door.

Seth's eyes widen. He jumps up and lets Ms. McLean enter. She's wearing yoga pants and a T-shirt, and I notice this because she isn't in the scrubs that I'm used to seeing her in. "Hi, boys. Some fresh-baked cookies? Compliments of Toll House."

"Yum," says Seth, taking three and then the plate, which he hands to me.

"Thank you." I grab one of the warm cookies.

"I'll just leave the plate with you two. Everything going okay?"

I nod.

Seth says, "Great."

Ms. McLean smiles. "It's so great that you have a friend over. And it's Charlie, no less."

"Okay, thanks. Bye, Mom," says Seth as he blushes, closing the door on her.

But now I'm wondering why Ms. McLean said that. I hadn't thought about the fact that I might not be the only one without friends. But Seth has an excuse: he's new to town.

"Good, huh?" he asks, eating his third cookie already.

I take a bite absentmindedly, but I don't respond. I'm having some stupid thoughts, like missing my mother, and worrying about having Seth as a friend, and screwing it up.

Seth cocks his head. "Something wrong?"

"Oh. No. Sorry."

"Eat up," he says, reaching for another cookie on the plate.

I take a bigger bite, and turn back to his photos. "The sunset one might be my favorite."

Between chews he says, "It's actually a sunrise. I like beginnings more than ends."

# BUT SOME DAYS ARE MADE
# FOR ENDINGS

•••••

Elation doesn't begin to describe my feelings after I hit my alarm this morning.

Yes, I, Charlie Dickens, have survived another school year. I am one year older. Wiser. (Ha!) And closer to being done with Whitehall, Montana, forever. Hallelujah. Amen.

This morning's sky is a picture I call *Hope Is a Million Golden Sunrays*.

Ms. Monakey has taken all the posters down. Her desk has only a pencil and a piece of paper on it. I think all this cleanup is a bit overkill for a summer vacation.

She's sitting at her desk with her head down, staring at her lap.

Being the only student in the classroom, I figure it's safe to talk to Ms. Monakey. "Where is everything?"

She looks to me with watery eyes. "I've been let go."

I try to fully understand the impact of that. "Fired?"

She nods and grabs a tissue. "I told myself not to get emotional today, but here I am." She blows her nose with a force that seems to shake her thin body.

"Why'd they fire you?"

Ms. Monakey is a great Spanish teacher. Even though, as I said before, she doesn't appear to have an ounce of Spanish in her.

"Budget cuts. They gave me a nice letter of recommendation." She weakly holds up the lone piece of paper from her desk.

I scan the room again. It's funny how different a classroom looks when it's empty. It's like it's missing a soul.

Seth walks into class and smiles at me. "Hey, Charlie." He slides into the desk behind me, and I turn to face him. Ms. Monakey sniffs, and dries her eyes with another tissue.

"What happened?" Seth asks.

"Fired," I whisper.

"No shit," says Seth. "That sucks."

"Possibly no Spanish class next year."

"I've been told worse things." Seth winks. "So, what are you doing to celebrate this momentous day?"

"Throwing a party," I deadpan. But I can't hold on to the seriousness of my statement, and a smile bursts forth. "Actually, probably going to take Tickles for a walk."

"Tickles?"

"Yeah. He's a dog."

"Who names a dog Tickles?"

"A six-year-old girl."

"Really?"

"Yeah, but she couldn't keep the dog." This is actually a story Geoffrey once told me.

"Can I come? I've always wanted a dog, but my mom's allergic. Or so she says. I have my suspicions that she's lying to avoid being pestered about getting a dog."

The one-minute warning bell rings. Students continue to walk into the classroom and then pause in the doorway as if they are in the wrong room. It's actually funny to watch.

"Anyway, walking a dog sounds like a celebration to me," Seth continues. "As long as we can get ice cream at some point."

"I haven't had ice cream in forever."

"What do you do with yourself, Charlie Dickens?"

"Laundry. Dishes. Homework."

"Well, it's time you live a little."

The class bell rings, and Ms. Monakey blows her nose before standing up from her desk. She makes her way to the front of the room. "All right, class," she says, not clasping her hands. "This is the day it ends."

# PAPERS FALLING FROM ROOFTOPS

•••••

The final bell rings. I am free! As I leave class, papers seem to fall from the sky, filling the hallway with assignments and homework—both graded and never-turned-in. Seth catches up to me as I kick papers out of my way, heading to my locker. I hate students who throw all their schoolwork at the final bell. It seems like a slap in the face to teachers who try to do some good in their students' lives. Plus, as lame as it sounds, I can't bring myself to litter like that. I can be so pathetic sometimes.

"It's chaos," Seth, coming toward me, yells over the screams and shouts.

"Did this happen at your old school?" I realize that I don't know anything about Seth's history.

Then it feels like a brick hits the side of my face. It stings. Slightly stunned, I hear laughing as papers flutter to the ground. I adjust my glasses.

Joey and Matt stand there. "Have a good summer, nerd," says Joey. "I hope you get some good writing done."

He throws another smaller stack of paper at me. He laughs, and Matt follows.

I'm walking away, thinking about how much I hate Joey and how I'm almost out of this damn building for three months, when I notice that Seth isn't next to me.

Oh shit.

He is right in Joey's face. "What's your problem? Your penis too small so you have to pick on people to make yourself feel bigger?"

"Listen, new kid, you better back off before you create a problem you don't want to have," says Joey, straightening up and puffing out his chest.

"Oh yeah? I'm not afraid of you or your loser friend." Seth scoops up some of the papers from the floor and chucks them at Joey's face.

Joey charges at Seth but halts when a deep voice booms from down the hall. "You two. Over here. Now." The principal, a demanding man who always wears a dark blue button-up shirt and khaki pants, points to his side.

Both Seth and Joey walk down the hall to the principal. I try to hang around for as long as possible, staring at the stupid sports trophy case like it interests me. I'm craning my neck, trying to hear what the principal is saying. But shortly afterward they head to the principal's office, and it gets too obvious that I'm loitering. So I walk outside. To loiter some more. The grass is so green, the sky so blue. I am ready to start summer, but I can't leave the school until I know Seth is okay.

I find myself sitting on the grass as the parking lot empties. I am twisting grass blades in my hands until they tear.

The world seems surprisingly empty at this moment. Few cars. Light traffic. No people. No birds. Or insect sounds. Just the occasional flutter of leaves.

Finally the door opens, and out walks Seth. His forehead is creased and his lips pursed. I stand up immediately. "What happened?"

"That dick Joey. He outright lied."

"Figures. He's a wuss."

"I have detention." Seth looks at me.

"But school's over." I don't understand how that works. Is there such a thing as summer detention?

"I know." He strides past me. I grab my backpack and catch up with him. "I start next year with a week of detention."

"Shit. I'm sorry."

"Don't be." Seth stops and turns to me. He seems so serious that I'm not sure if it's the same Seth. "I will not let anyone pick on you. Or do anything to you. I swear, Charlie. I will kick that kid's ass. He's lucky the principal stopped things when he did."

I'm speechless, and I don't think a "thanks" would cover it. So, like an idiot, I keep quiet.

Seth walks to the parking lot, and loses all the seriousness he just had. "Let's go walk a dog," he says. Then laughs. "A dog with the worst name in the history of dogs."

# THE WALK OF THE LITTLE ROBOT DOG

•••••

Standing on the front porch of Geoffrey's house, I'm about to knock, when I stop and say, "Oh. One thing. Geoffrey is quite . . . large. So there's that."

Seth smiles. His camera hangs around his neck, becoming almost like a comfort to see.

I knock and enter, and Seth follows me inside.

Geoffrey is snoring loudly on his green, less-newish love seat. I look at Seth, and his eyes are wide in amazement. I turn back to Geoffrey and clear my throat. That does nothing to wake him, and I always feel awkward about waking people up anyway. So I wonder if we should just come back later. Though, the next thing I know, Seth is racing across the living room and catching Geoffrey's laptop as it slides off his belly. Geoffrey wakes up with Seth standing next to him, one hand holding his laptop. Geoffrey screams in terror, and Seth looks startled.

I step toward them and say, "It's just me."

Geoffrey turns his head and finally looks like he

recognizes something in this world of his. He puts his hands down and tries to adjust his massive frame on the couch. It's a bit of a struggle.

"Scared me half to death." Geoffrey puts his hand to his heart. "Still beating, so that's good." He coughs.

"Sorry for scaring you," I say. "This is my friend, Seth."

Seth nods and hands Geoffrey his laptop. "Was just trying to save your computer from falling."

Geoffrey takes the computer. To be honest, he seems slightly out of it.

"We're going to walk Tickles," I say.

Geoffrey nods.

"Tickles!" I shout. His little bell gets louder as he comes from the back bedroom.

Seth's eyes grow wide again. "Whoa. Is that a fake leg?"

"Oh yeah," I say. "I forgot to tell you that Tickles had a run-in with a car once. The car won."

"That leg is awesome," he says.

"Ready for a walk?" I ask. Tickles jumps up onto my leg, and his tail wags.

"Seems like Tickles is doing pretty good for himself," says Seth. I kneel to connect the leash to the collar. As I'm petting Tickles, I hear a *click* and turn to see Seth also kneeling with his camera pointed at me. "Can't waste a good moment."

"Uh." I stand. "I'm not used to having my picture taken."

"Sometimes I get involved in a shot and forget to ask if it's okay to take it. Is it okay?"

"You already took it." If he wants pictures of me, I guess I don't care. In a way, it is flattering. But kind of frightening, too, like my life is always one random moment away from being on display for the town to mock. Or being captured, possibly forever.

Geoffrey says, "No pictures of me." He coughs. "My mom would die if she saw me this big."

"Well, I'd never show her, then." Seth smiles at Geoffrey.

"Where is your mom?" I ask. "In Whitehall?"

Geoffrey chuckles. "Oh, no. Vermont. Tiny little city. Before you go, have a cookie. Judy made them. I think they're chocolate chip." There's a plate of homemade cookies, with a sizable portion of cookies missing from one side, on the coffee table next to Geoffrey.

"Oh, awesome," says Seth, smiling. "I love cookies." As he eats, he asks, "Is Judy your wife?"

I explain to Seth that Judy is the woman who helps Geoffrey with chores and taking a shower and things around the house. She's also the one who goes to the store for him. Seth nods. "May I?" He grabs another cookie.

As Seth and I make our way down the street, cookies in hand and Tickles in tow—or rather, leading with his little legs, bell ringing—Seth turns to me. "He is huge. Reminds me of this show I watched called *My 600 lb. Life*. But the irony was that the people on the show didn't have much of a life until they lost, like, half of themselves in weight. Like, this one girl never got out of bed, all because it hurt her knees to move. How much do you think he weighs? Can he walk, or is he stuck on the couch?"

"Not sure and not sure." I take a bite of the cookie.

"It stinks really bad in there."

"I didn't notice. Maybe I'm used to it? He's lived there

for about five years. He was pretty big when he moved in, but in the past five years he's probably doubled in size."

Seth shakes his head. "I'd love to document someone like him."

"A movie?" I ask.

Seth holds up the camera around his neck.

"That would be cool, but he'd never let you."

"Seriously, how much do you think he weighs?"

"Probably around six hundred pounds." It's a guess, but probably not off by much.

Seth watches Tickles for a minute. "That dog can move. He's like a little robot dog."

I smirk. Little robot dog.

We decide to walk Tickles through town and not on the dirt road. With new company, a different route seems to be in order. Tickles doesn't seem to mind the shake-up in the routine either.

"Want to hold the leash?" I ask.

"Yes!" Seth puts out his hand. "Did I mention that I want a dog? I think I mentioned that."

"I think you did," I say with a smirk.

We make it to the corner of the street, and Seth holds Tickles back from darting into traffic. We don't want Tickles to lose another leg. Bad joke, but it's true. A loud diesel truck revs by, and a thick black cloud of exhaust consumes us. Tickles shakes from the noise as he hides behind my leg. "We should probably pick him up and cross and go to a less busy street."

"D-bags," says Seth. "I hate those trucks that don't have exhaust filters."

"They should be illegal."

"Totally. Like throw-their-ass-in-jail-for-killing-the-planet illegal."

"Do you want to pick up Tickles? Or want me to?"

Seth quickly takes off his camera. "Can you hold this?"

I'm waiting for him to tell me to protect his camera with my life, or something equally dramatic. And when people say those things, aren't they basically saying that the object they hand you is worth the same (or more) than your life? And isn't that stupid? But Seth doesn't say anything like that. He holds the camera out to me, and I nervously take it and put the strap around my neck, and even hold the camera with one hand. I want to protect it with my life anyway.

Tickles sitting in Seth's arms is actually pretty cute, and if I knew how to work his complex professional-looking camera, I would take a picture. "How do I take a picture?"

He puts his hand out and touches the button. "Push that button down and twist that little handle thing next to it toward you." I do. And the camera turns on. "Then just look, aim, and press that same button."

*Snap.*

Seth holds a shivering Tickles. "Funny how I don't get many pictures with myself." We cross the street. "Then again, I'm the least interesting subject I know."

Once we reach the other side of the street, Seth puts Tickles down.

"Let's walk to the park. Just down this street," I say.

"You're the boss."

As we walk, every few seconds Seth clears his throat like he has something caught in it. Tickles seems to have forgotten about the truck and runs ahead of us again.

Just happy to move his little legs. Bell still ringing.

Seth rubs his eyes.

"Everything okay?" I ask.

He clears his throat. "Fine."

By the time we reach the park, everything is no longer fine. Seth looks like his face is going to explode: it's red and puffy. He is having a hard time breathing and can't talk. He's strangling.

I realize I need to get him to the hospital. Fast.

I help him sit down and then look around for someone to help, all the while hearing Seth choke on nothing. I see a person on the far side of the park, and I wave my hands and shout—until I realize I have a phone. Adrenaline makes it hard for me to think sometimes. My fingers shake nervously, and it seems to take forever to find and press three numbers. It's like I have forgotten how to function.

"Hold on," I tell him as I grab the leash. "Breathe. Just breathe."

But he isn't doing that very well. And his eyes look scared, which makes me worry more. "It'll be okay," I tell him. But I'm not sure. Tickles sits down on the sidewalk, unaware that anything bad is happening.

"Nine-one-one emergency. How may I help you?"

The first thing out of my mouth is "I need help!" But isn't that rather obvious and stupid to say when you've called 911? I'm wasting time that I can't afford to waste.

And Seth's eyes only grow in fear.

# CLOSE ENCOUNTERS

•••••

My world stopped when Seth was choking on air. I don't know what I would've done if he had died in front of me. But luckily, that didn't happen.

Whoever invented epinephrine is my new hero.

It's late, but Seth is home and in bed. He fell asleep immediately, which I take as my sign to leave. I'm walking down the stairs with Ms. McLean. "Charlie," she says. "Thank you very much for taking care of Seth today."

"I'm sorry for what happened. I didn't know he was allergic to peanuts. I didn't even know those cookies had peanuts in them."

Ms. McLean follows me to the door. "Well, you were a great friend for sticking next to him. I don't know how I can ever repay you for that."

I bite my lip slightly and hesitate. "Dinner."

"You want dinner?"

I nod.

"We can do that. How about Sunday night?"

"Really? Oh, that'd be great." I wasn't thinking she'd be so willing to cook right away. I figure she'd do that adult thing where they say something like, "Of course. Let's get together soon." And soon never comes. I am so excited. I can't remember the last time I had a real home-cooked meal.

"What do you like?" she asks.

"Ribs."

"Okay."

"And corn."

She smiles.

"And corn bread," I add.

"I think we can make that happen."

"And beans."

She laughs, and I'm not sure what compels me, but I find myself hugging Ms. McLean. I want to say thank you, but she says it first. And a thank-you after a thank-you seems awkward.

I pull away and then feel embarrassed for hugging her.

The lights are off at home, and I pause at the sidewalk. I stare a second or two longer at my house and its bleakness. It's really bothering me that I can't share my day with my dad. He'll be out with friends at the bowling alley until late. He's in a league. But I'm pretty sure it's just an excuse to drink and not be home.

I don't even make dinner. I just head upstairs and fall onto my bed, letting out a big sigh. It's the first night in a long while that I'm too tired to even look out my window. I still suspect that if any UFO comes by tonight, I'll be able to hear it or see it. Though, it was one heck of a day, so I hope the aliens won't actually come around tonight, so that I can get a good night's sleep first.

Lying on top of my covers, clothes still on, I think about how much I'm looking forward to spending my summer with Seth. Maybe this will be the summer I can do some things that I could never really do alone, at least without being teased. Like going bowling. Or going to a movie.

In my mind, I'm in my brand-new Ford F-250, driving Seth down the main street with all the little old storefronts. It's a bright sunny day, and we're heading to an afternoon matinee. I parallel park with ease.

We come upon Jennifer Bennett and her friends standing outside the movie theater. I'm cool and composed.

"Hey, JB," I say. "Join us for the movie?"

Seth looks at me with wide-eyed amazement. He can't believe Charlie Dickens is talking to her. Is asking this.

JB gazes at me with stars in her eyes. "I'd love to." She holds out her hand, and I take it.

That'd be the day, wouldn't it? I crawl under my covers, thinking about all the ways I can be a superhero in my real life. Talking to Jennifer Bennett constitutes one major way.

# A HARD FALL AND SORRY

.....

With my shoulders tense, I take a deep breath and knock. The door swings opens, and Seth stands there.

I gulp. "Hi."

"Hi," he says.

"You look like yourself."

Seth laughs. "I hope so."

I shake my head. "I mean, you look so much better than the other night."

"The night I almost died, you mean?"

I clear my throat. "Yeah. That night."

I stand there. In my nicer clothes. He stands there. In shorts and a T-shirt. Looking at me.

"Why you all dressed up?"

I suddenly regret wanting to dress up. But I wanted to make a special evening out of the fact that I'm having a home-cooked meal, which I haven't had in a long, long time.

"Uh, I don't know."

Seth chuckles and steps aside, saying, "Come on in, Charlie."

I move my shaking knees into the house. We head right to the table, and Ms. McLean—er, Susan—walks in with a plate of corn on the cob. "Just in time, Charlie. And look at you, all fancy like. Looking good."

She sits down, and I look around the dark wood table at the ribs, corn bread, and now the steaming corn on the cob.

"This looks delicious."

Susan turns to Seth. "At least someone appreciates my cooking."

Seth rolls his eyes.

I take some of everything and begin to tear into the ribs. Barbecue sauce covers my lips and around my mouth, but it's too good to wipe off right away.

Both Seth and Susan are smirking at me.

"Sorry." I put the ribs down and wipe my mouth.

"No, dig in. It's nice to see someone devour my food," Susan says.

Seth picks at the corn bread with his fingers. He flashes a look at his mom.

"Are you all packed?" Susan asks him.

"Almost."

"I don't want a repeat of last year, speeding down the highway at ninety miles an hour so you won't miss your flight."

"Where you going?" I ask.

"Visiting my dad in Seattle."

Susan wipes her mouth. "He goes for three weeks every summer."

The news is like a punch to my gut. It hurts.

Three weeks? What I thought would be a summer of fun and adventure with Seth has quickly turned into a summer of feeling oddly abandoned. "That sounds like fun." I try to sound enthused when I'm decidedly not.

"It'll be good," Seth says.

*Keep calm, Charlie.* Three weeks from now will be just after the Fourth of July weekend—not even halfway through summer. I tell myself it'll be okay. Seth will be back in no time. Plus I have work, Tickles, Grandma, and my own UFO research and maybe (hopefully) seeing and hanging out with the girl of my dreams, Jennifer Bennett.

"Yes, it'll be good," I repeat.

I put the napkin on my empty plate. "That was delicious, Ms. McLean."

"Charlie. I keep telling you to call me 'Susan.' And thank you." She stands, grabs the empty plates, and goes through the kitchen door.

"Sorry. Susan."

"Want to go up to my room?" asks Seth.

"Sure."

Seth sits at his computer desk. I look around his room again as if I had forgotten how cool it is. Seth turns to me. "What are you looking at?"

"Looks like you really are packed." He has two big suitcases sitting near his bed.

"Yeah. I'm bringing all my camera equipment. So hopefully I'll get some good pictures in Seattle. If I do, I'll send you some."

My heart jumps. "That'd be great. Yeah, please do."

I might be a tad too excited about this. But that means he wants to at least keep in touch. I won't be completely alone.

"I need to finish editing this one before I go," he says. On the monitor is the picture of me pulling my grandma up from her chair. It's black and white. A tender, beautiful moment frozen in time.

"I love it," Seth says. "It's a picture about love." He's facing the monitor as he clicks things and changes settings on the picture.

"A picture about love," I repeat. "I like that."

Seth turns to me. "Don't you mean you *love* it?" He chuckles, and turns and does a few more clicks. "There. Done. What do you think?"

It's so perfect and beautiful, and even has this magical feeling between our faces, that I don't have the words to describe it.

A piece of thick cardstock feeds into the printer on his desk.

"You're printing it?"

"You can't hang it up from my computer, can you?"

"But . . ."

He hands me the photograph and catches my eyes. It feels very personal. "You're welcome." Seth smiles, and I'm truly shocked by his kindness.

"Thank you." Without thinking, I sit on his bed, which then feels like I disregarded someone's personal space. I maybe should've asked. But Seth doesn't seem to mind or notice. In fact, he sits next to me.

"So, my mom told me you visit your grandma like almost every day. That's super impressive."

"Not every day. But—"

"Hold that thought." Seth jumps up and turns on his bedside lamp and turns off his overhead light. "Much better." He scoots up to the headboard of his bed and pats the bed next to him.

I look at him.

"Well, don't be afraid. I won't attack. This time." He winks.

I scoot up to his headboard and sit next to him. It all feels even more personal. But I guess this is what friends do together. Personal things. "So, you were saying?" he asks.

"Yeah." I study the photograph. "My dad and I are all she has left. I'm kind of the end of the Dickens line." I take a deep breath. "I worry that if I don't visit her, she'll be forgotten. She'll be nobody because even she doesn't know who she is. That leaves a shell of a person. I mean, are you even a person if you don't know who you are?"

I can feel Seth staring at me. My eyes stay glued to the photograph, even though I'm no longer studying it.

"Wow. That's pretty deep, Charlie." Seth puts his hands behind his head. "That may be one of the smartest things anyone has ever said to me."

I finally break my gaze from the photograph. "It's not."

"New rule," he says. "Every time you say something shitty about yourself, you get a punch."

"I don't like that rule."

"Tough. We're going to get you to stop demeaning yourself. It's like you're sorry for your existence or something."

Those words also feel like a punch to the stomach. I'm getting mentally beat up tonight, and I think it's my own doing.

After a while Ms. McLean calls up that Seth needs to get to bed. "Early flight," she says.

"Ugh," Seth says.

"Ugh," I echo, though I think we're ughing for different reasons.

Seth smiles. "Ugh. Am I right?"

"Right," I say. "Ugh."

Soon we're laughing at all the "right" and ughing we're doing, and then Seth gets all serious. "I'll miss you, Charlie."

I stand up from his bed and say, "Yeah. Have fun in Seattle with your dad." I want to say "I'll miss you too," but I fear it'll sound weird and make me too vulnerable.

"Charlie." Seth stands up and puts his hands on my shoulders. "You have my number. Let's stay in touch. I'll be back before we know it, and then we can go on summer adventures."

I nod. That is the best thing I could've heard. "A summer full of adventures."

"A summer full of them," Seth echoes back.

# PART TWO

## STITCHING TOGETHER A HORIZON

# THE PROBABLY
# IMPROBABLE MISSION

•••••

I wake up on the first Monday of summer at ten a.m. It's fantastic. I get up and stretch and go to my desk—which, like everything I own, is pathetically incomparable to Seth's—and check the Montana UFO site. It has been updated with the following information:

> Spotted on Sunday night around midnight
>
> (approx.) in Whitehall, MT: a loud buzz
>
> followed by a blinding bright flash.
>
> Reported by Charlie D.

I massage my temples. What a mess this turned out to be, with wanting validation and ending up being the source on the event.

My phone buzzes. Hey, made it to Seattle. I forgot how much I love big cities.

I don't know what to say to that. My only time in a big city was when we drove to Salt Lake City when I was ten.

All I remember is the long car ride, because we didn't even do anything fun while we were there. Except for eat at a cool Japanese restaurant where they made the food right in front of you. But at least my mom was with me then. I think I would've enjoyed everything so much more if I had known that my mom wouldn't always be around. But I guess that's a lot to understand as a kid.

I text back, I wouldn't know. But small towns suck!

I wait for a response, but after a few minutes of staring and suddenly feeling stupid about it, I put my phone into my pocket and go downstairs. In the kitchen I pour some orange juice, and as I stand at the counter drinking it, I wonder what the hell I am going to do with my time/day/summer.

The clock ticks.

*Tick.*

*Tick.*

I eat breakfast and think about how I have to essentially entertain myself, which sucks, because up until yesterday, I thought Seth would be around. As a kid, I could use my imagination. I could spend hours and hours by myself with only a few toys, or a branch from a tree, or my bike. Nowadays I get bored so easily.

The kitchen looks so worn, the wallpaper peeling at the edges. I bring the bowl to the sink. The house just sits here. Stagnant. Cold. How can everything feel so immovable when the earth is spinning at a rate of a thousand miles per hour?

I feel a walk would do me good, and so I walk into town and past the newspaper building. The *Whitehall Courier* is something of a weekly gossip rag. It's well known that

Jennifer Bennett works at the newspaper, as she tends to write weekly news stories that get featured on the first or second page of the paper. I try to read all her stories. She is going to go places in life—and none of them will be in Whitehall.

I casually glance in the windows as I walk past, to see if I can catch a glimpse of her working. Maybe I could go in and talk to her? But the sun's reflection off the glass blinds me, so I can't see inside. Irritated at my lack of courage, I decide that I have a summer mission while Seth is gone, which I dub Mission Probably Improbable: Date Jennifer Bennett.

Step one of said mission: talk to her.

I'm heading in the direction of my work, when I realize I should've stopped by Geoffrey's to get Tickles. He would've enjoyed the walk.

I take a right at the main junction—the only one in Whitehall with a flashing red light that is hung by wire across the intersection. As I turn the corner, I run right into my favorite group of assholes: the Ass Trio. This definitely sucks. And only day one of summer. And no Seth.

They are clearly loitering in front of the town's grocery store. And frankly, the manager should have them all arrested. I would if I were the manager. And if I were the town sheriff, I'd kick them out of town and never let them return, just like they used to do in the Old West.

"Oh, look! Little Charles Dickens is out of his study," says Joey.

I put my head down and try to walk around him, but he grabs hold of my arm.

"Not so fast," he says. "Stay and chat a little."

Psych licks an ice cream cone.

"Where's your boyfriend?" asks Joey.

Both Matt and Psych laugh.

"Yeah, where is he?" echoes Matt.

Psych takes another lick of his ice cream cone.

I try to pull out of Joey's grip so that I can leave, but he holds me more tightly. "He got me detention next year. That wasn't very nice of him. I kind of want to kick his ass, but he's not here. So maybe I should just kick yours instead?"

"Just let me go. I have to get to work." That's a lie, but it seems like something I should say to get out of here.

Joey pulls at my arm and yanks me toward him. "Not so fast. I'm not done—"

"Joey, what are you doing?"

I turn my head quickly when I hear that voice. My heartbeat quickens.

Joey holds on to me as he turns to her. "Just talking to my friend here."

Jennifer Bennett stares at me, as if trying to figure out if what she sees lines up with what Joey said. I jerk my arm free from Joey's grip.

Oh my god. She just saw me being roughed up by Joey. I can't even defend myself, which is not attractive. My chance of getting with Jennifer Bennett just decreased exponentially from my already low odds. My face burns red, and as usual around Jennifer Bennett, I want to disappear.

"What are you doing?" Joey asks her.

"Going to work," she says. "Why don't you find something better to do with your time and leave Charlie alone?"

I can't believe that Jennifer Bennett is saving me from being bullied for a second time in my life. I want to say thank you, but I don't think that's a smart move at this moment.

Now, you might be wondering why Joey would even

listen to Jennifer Bennett. It's simple: he likes her. Like, really likes her. She knows it because he isn't shy about saying things, but nothing has ever happened between them.

Thank god.

"Well . . . yeah. Duh," he says. "Like I said, we were just talking. Ain't that right, buddy?" Joey turns to me.

Jennifer Bennett raises her eyebrows skeptically, and then she says to him, "Maybe you should go read a book, give yourself something to do."

Joey starts to say, "Like one by my favorite—"

"Don't even start, Joey. It's not even the same name." Jennifer Bennett starts to walk away. "Good-bye, boys."

I stand there dumbfounded as the Ass Trio all say bye to her, and Joey shouts out, "What are you doing Friday? How about a movie and . . . some after-movie fun?" Matt and Psych laugh like the asses they are. Jennifer just waves without looking back.

They wait until she turns the corner, but I have already darted across the street, and I hear Joey shout out to me, "We're not done talking, Dickens. And next time bring your boyfriend! I want to kick his ass!"

Sometimes I wish I had some kind of alien laser gun that would just obliterate people from this planet. They'd be transported to another dimension. Or another planet far away. I can imagine Joey wandering around, scared, on some red-earthed surface as a ravenous wind beats dust against his ragged body. No matter how far he travels, he wouldn't recognize anyone or anything. One minute he'd be picking on little Charlie Dickens, and the next he'd be light-years away. Forever.

And did I just refer to myself as "little Charlie Dickens"? *Come on, Charlie, you can do better.*

# ANOTHER PLACE TO FIND

•••••

The sun has set on the horizon, the big sky etching into darkness. I lie in my bed, staring at the white popcorn ceiling, trying to discern faces or animals. The room grows darker and darker until the house sits quietly in the darkness of the world. But I have an idea.

The stairs creak as I walk down to the living room. The same blue light emits from the TV, silhouetting my dad as he sits reclined in his chair. The volume on the TV is so low that I almost don't think he can be watching.

My dad, without turning around, says, "Where are you going, Charlie?"

I freeze. "How do you know I'm going anywhere?"

"Because I wasn't born yesterday."

"Just going out."

"What does that mean?" My dad has yet to look at me.

"Going to go take a walk."

"It's pitch-black out."

"I just want to get some fresh air. My room is stuffy."

He finally turns around to face me on the stairs. "You're not searching for some UFO thing, right? You know they don't exist. Not only is it a waste of your time, but you know what would happen to us if the town thought you were anything like your crazy mother."

I just stand there. I don't believe him. She wasn't crazy, and aliens do exist. They have to.

"Huh?" he asks more loudly.

"No."

He eyes me suspiciously. "When are you going to let it go? It's been years. Why don't you come have a seat on the couch. We can watch something."

"Right now?"

"Yes. Now. You never want to chill with your old man anymore."

I put my backpack by the stairs and go sit on the couch with my jacket on. We both sit in the blue glow and the hushed sounds of the TV. Neither one of us speaks.

He watches reruns of something called *The Red Green Show* on PBS. He takes sips from a can of beer.

I twiddle my thumbs.

Good family time, Dad.

"See, isn't this fun?"

I yawn. "I think I'm going to go to bed." I stand up.

"Why don't you come bowling with me and the guys this week?"

"Uh." I stand there wondering why I am being invited.

"What do you say?" He seems genuinely excited about having me join him. I'm confused by that. I always figured bowling was his attempt to get away.

"Uhhh . . . Yeah?"

"Yeah? Good."

I grab my backpack and walk up the creaky stairs to my bedroom. I sit on my bed and let out a sigh.

Why does he care if I look for UFOs? It's not like I'm going to shout that fact out to the world.

It happened as I sat crouched by the window in my room during fifth grade, and he walked in. I was holding binoculars, and he said, "What are you trying to see in the dark?"

I looked at him, back to the window, and back to him. "Uh . . ."

"Don't tell me your mother has gotten to you?" He walked up to me and kneeled. "Aliens aren't real, Charlie. And whatever she says is false."

"But Mom says—"

"I don't give a damn what your mother says. Stop this nonsense. Here's some money for a basketball." Money was particularly tight for us. Mom wasn't working.

At that time, I was only periodically looking for UFOs. It was a hobby at best.

But now it's so much more. Because now she's with them.

I'm getting pissed that he never believed her and now thinks I'm crazy too. I look out my window and decide that he's not going to keep me inside. I grab my backpack and open the window. I maneuver onto the roof below and then the tree that's to the left of my room.

Soon I'm walking the cracked sidewalk, wondering if I should get Tickles. But Geoffrey's house is dark. I look back at the tiny blue light coming from our front room window.

The woods that lie so close to my house have a quiet maliciousness at night. But I've grown up next to them, so I am aware of what lies beyond. I enter the forest of pine trees and wander through until I start my climb up to the top of a hill. I have a flashlight with me, as even a full moon's light can't fully penetrate through the trees to the bouncy, needle-thick ground.

When I reach the top of the hill, I find what I was looking for: a barren patch of land with two massive, flat-top rocks. I climb one of the rocks, lie on my back, and put the backpack behind my head. I observe the crystal clear sky and watch the stars. I scan the darkness for fragments of light. Moving light is really what I want to catch, but just because the light moves doesn't mean it's a UFO, and just because the light doesn't move doesn't mean it's not a UFO. UFOs can be tricky—especially when they don't want to be seen.

If I don't see a UFO, I at least hope to see a shooting star. I've seen dozens in my life, and I don't think I'll ever get tired of seeing them. Every time I see one shoot across the sky, I watch in awe like it's the first time.

Flashes of Jennifer Bennett rescuing me earlier today flood my mind. I'd like to thank her just so I could have a reason to talk to her, but now I'm super embarrassed because she saved me from getting my ass kicked. How can I ever come back from the humiliation that I can't stick up for myself? How could a girl ever like a guy like that?

I will never get a chance with her, and I am sick

of thinking that someday everything will be different. Nothing ever really changes in my life or around Whitehall. It's frustrating because it feels like everyone is always trying to keep me down.

I stand up and look straight up to the sky. I put my arms out and I shout, "I'm here! Come get me!"

I'm ready to be taken. I'm ready for a new life. One where I am not so awkward. One without all the responsibilities. One with a whole new set of possibilities. One where I can be with my mom.

"Please! Come get me! I'm ready!"

My gaze doesn't leave the sky, but nothing happens. I drop my arms and then lie back down on the rock.

Still watching the sky, my back on the cool rock, I manage to fall asleep.

# THE WORLD SPINS SO QUICKLY, BUT TIME CAN STILL STOP

. . . . .

After waking up sometime in the middle of the night, I hurriedly walk home, hoping my dad has gone to bed, because I can't get back up to my room the same way I got down.

But I'm not that lucky.

The TV is still playing, and the sound is still low, and my dad is still in the recliner. "You're in big trouble, young man," he says as I enter the house.

He pulls the recliner handle back so that the footrest folds back into the chair, and he stands up. He faces me, his eyes heavy. "It's . . ." He looks at his watch. "Nearly three."

"I wasn't doing anything bad. I just . . . fell asleep outside."

"You purposely disobeyed me by sneaking out. You're grounded."

"Whatever," I say, as I trudge upstairs.

"Watch your tone. Now get to bed!" he yells after me.

My dad is the worst at parenting. Seriously. My life won't change at all with my dad's "grounding." For one, he's never home enough to actually follow through with any punishments. He also doesn't really know what to ground me from. He'd keep me home, except he's always wanting me to go out and make some friends, almost as if his own social life depends on not having an outcast for a son. If my dad could ground me from anything, it'd be from staying inside or searching for UFOs. But history shows he has no luck with either. So he doesn't even try.

I slam my door shut, just to show that it's me who isn't happy with him.

Geoffrey shrugs after he hears my story. "You know, my dad never understood me much, either." Geoffrey coughs, and his face turns slightly blue.

I scoot up to the edge of the recliner, ready to stand and do something for him. "Everything okay?"

He puts his hand over his chest and hits it a few times. Finally the coughing subsides. "Fine. I'm fine."

"You . . . might want to get that looked at?"

Geoffrey nods, but he doesn't appear to be concerned. When I walked into Geoffrey's house a few minutes ago, I could smell some sour odor—almost like rotting urine. I think it's the same thing Seth smelled, only it's stronger now.

Tickles's bell rings by my feet. He was sitting by my foot, but he keeps standing up, walking in a circle, and sitting down. He repeats it again and again.

"I think Tickles is ready for a walk," Geoffrey finally manages to say.

The sun burns through Geoffrey's living room window. I enjoy the brightness, but he says, "Can you close the blinds for me?"

Tickles follows me over to the blinds, and I suddenly think about the time when Seth and I went walking with Tickles, and Seth had an allergic reaction. He didn't know he was that allergic to peanuts. The doctor said allergies can sometimes get more severe over time.

I check my phone. Nothing from Seth.

Before I leave, I turn to Geoffrey and say, "Need anything while I'm out?"

He coughs once and says, "How about some cough syrup?"

I nod, and as I begin to close the front door, he shouts, "Oh, and some ice cream."

I return later with his supplies, and as I walk in, I notice a pained and frightened look on Geoffrey's face. "Charlie." I also can smell the same sickly sour smell, but somehow it managed to get even stronger since the walk.

"What's wrong?" I rush over to him.

He tries to sit up straighter. He looks at me and says, "I need you to do me a huge favor. Only for a couple of days."

"Anything." I don't like where this conversation is heading.

"I need you to watch Tickles while I'm in the hospital. I figure you're the best person for him."

"Hospital?"

Geoffrey nods, his massive second chin shaking. "Just for a few days. Need to get a couple of tests. I'm leaving later today. When the ambulance gets here."

"Holy crap. Is there anything I can do?"

Geoffrey coughs. "Don't worry about me. I'll be fine. It's Tickles I'm worried about."

I shake my head. "Don't be. Seriously. He's in great hands."

Geoffrey smiles. "Thank you, Charlie." He coughs again. "He can even stay at your place if that's more convenient for you."

I'm not entirely sure what is going on with Geoffrey. But I'm scared.

I sit down on the recliner, suddenly aware of how at one point Geoffrey sat in this same seat until he became too massive to fit comfortably. I wonder what it would be like to be so large that this recliner wouldn't hold me. That would be such a different life that I can't even process my thoughts on it. How could someone allow themselves to get so big? Wouldn't even a daily walk fight against becoming basically immobile?

"Charlie?" asks Geoffrey.

"Yes?"

"Can you stay until the ambulance gets here?" He coughs again.

"Maybe we can watch something on the History Channel?" I say, getting situated in the recliner. I know it's his favorite channel.

# TRANSPORT

.....

When the two ambulance guys arrive, they stare at Geoffrey in shock. I don't think they were expecting such a big guy. "Can you walk?" asks one of them. "Our gurney isn't large enough."

Geoffrey nods, but his face expresses doubt.

The stockier of the two guys says, "Let's call for help. Just in case."

Geoffrey coughs and coughs and coughs as the two ambulance guys go outside. One stands near the ambulance with a phone up to his ear. He turns and looks at the house.

After another thirty minutes—good thing no one is dying—an emergency unit truck from the fire department arrives. Two guys jump out, and all four men huddle together outside. It looks like they're talking logistics.

Geoffrey asks me what's happening. "Uh. I think they're trying to figure out what to do."

"How to get me out?"

"Uh. Yeah."

I'm standing back, out of the way, as all four men—wearing gloves—pull Geoffrey up to his feet on a count of three.

Once up, his legs wobble. The fat deposits on his stomach and legs make him look off-kilter and asymmetrical. After he stands, that sour odor I've been smelling erupts into the room, and it is then that I realize something: Geoffrey stopped getting up to go to the bathroom.

As he stands there, one ambulance man on each side holding him up, he looks so sad. He looks small, and I don't mean his body but something about him. His essence or being. His head lowers in shame, and his legs continue to tremble. "Let's walk," says the same ambulance guy who called for help. I follow a few steps behind, with Tickles on a leash. The back door is open, but I notice that Geoffrey looks wider than the width of the door. The younger ambulance guy glances behind Geoffrey to the older guy.

"We measured. You can make it, but you're going to have to squeeze," says the older one to Geoffrey.

Geoffrey doesn't respond.

After they load him into the ambulance, I have to pick Tickles up because he keeps trying to jump into the ambulance. I hold him as he shivers in my arms.

"Take good care of him," says Geoffrey, covered in sweat.

"I promise," I say. "We'll come visit you."

Geoffrey smiles weakly as they close the back doors to the ambulance. I hear coughing before the ambulance starts and drives off. Tickles still shivers in my arms. "It's okay. It'll all be okay," I whisper to him. And I hope I'm right.

# A SHOT IN THE DARK

.....

After he goes around sniffing the house and furniture, Tickles relaxes. I put him in my room with water and food and his doggie bed, and close the door. I don't want my dad to come home and find a dog before I'm able to talk to him.

Watching Tickles sniff his doggie bed before walking around it a couple of times and sitting, I think about how fantastic it'd be to own a dog.

Tickles barks, and I put my finger over my lips. "Shhh. No barking."

I was riding my bike in the street. I was maybe in fourth grade. Occasionally I'd ride to the far end of the street and see the road stretch in front of me for what seemed like forever.

"You are cleared for takeoff on runway six," I'd say out loud.

"Roger. Runway six," I'd reply in a different voice.

I'd hit imaginary buttons, and then I'd start pedaling faster.

Faster.

Faster still.

I'd imagine lifting off the ground. Climbing. Higher. Higher.

Away from the earth.

But this particular time, as I pedaled at top speed, I noticed an odd sight: a truck coming at me. I screeched my bike to a stop and watched this large U-Haul turn into the driveway next to ours.

I rode closer to the house and watched as the truck door opened and out came a large man. Followed by a four-legged tiny, brown curly-haired dog. "Hello," the man said, and waved at me.

I watched the dog run around and sniff various things—the truck tires, the fence. Finally he ran up to me and sniffed at my shoe and bike. He acted as if he had been locked away his entire life.

I looked back to the man. "Are you moving in?"

"Yep."

"I live there." I pointed to the house next to his.

"I'll be your new neighbor, then. I'm Geoffrey."

I felt something warm on my leg, and by the time I looked down, the dog was already trotting off, acting like he hadn't even peed on someone's leg.

"Eww. Yuck."

The front door to my house creaked opened, and out came my mother in jeans and a knit sweater. "Charlie, come inside and quit bothering this man."

"His dog just peed on me," I said, looking at my mom.

"Sorry about that," said Geoffrey. "He's never done such a thing before. Must like you."

"I don't like him." I shook my leg to try to get some of the piss off.

"Tell you what," Geoffrey said. "Stop by sometime, and I'll give you some ice cream to make up for it."

My mom smiled.

"Only if the dog isn't around," I replied.

Geoffrey laughed, but I was serious.

I got on my bike and rode up to the garage with one yellow sock and a sticky ankle. I really didn't like that dog.

It's about five thirty. I have to leave for work in fifteen minutes, and I don't want to keep Tickles holed up in my bedroom. So I first decide to let it roam the house. But then I realize that he probably shouldn't, since he hasn't been around the house alone yet, and I don't want him to freak out. So I bring him back up to my room and close the door. On my way to work I stop by a bar called The Office, which is where my dad hangs out with his friends after their shift ends.

The bar is dark and smoky. Even though smoking in buildings is illegal, it doesn't stop certain people from doing it. And no one says anything. There's a line of guys laughing at the bar, all with dirty clothes. My dad is sitting between a couple of bigger guys. He takes a drink of his beer as I walk up behind him. He puts the beer on the counter and swivels.

"Charlie, what are you doing?" asks my dad. "You can't be in here." He doesn't even mention the grounding; he's probably forgotten about it.

"Hey, Charlie," says Ted, one of my dad's friends. "Gettin' tall."

"It's Geoffrey's dog," I say to my dad. "We need to keep him at our house for a few days."

"Why?"

"Geoffrey had to go to the hospital and needs someone to take care of Tickles. He asked me."

"Then go to his house and take care of the dog like you've basically done for a year now." He takes another gulp of his beer. "Now get out of here before you get in trouble."

"Please. Why can't he just stay at our house?"

"I'm sorry to hear about Geoffrey," says my dad. "But no dogs." With that, my dad turns back around to face the bar. But I'm not done with this.

I'm mopping behind the counter at around seven thirty p.m. when the door dings and I look over. "John!" I have continually felt bad for brushing him off in the middle of his story the night Seth and Susan showed up. I want to make it up to him. "Glad you're back."

John takes off his hat, uses his hand to comb his hair over, and shuffles over to the counter. "Why, that's mighty kind of you to say," says John. His eyebrows and mustache are as thick as ever. I bet John would make a great grandpa. I never really knew mine. My mom's parents live far away in Indiana, and my dad's dad—Harold—died when I was little.

John heaves himself into a seat and says, "Coffee, cream, and eggs, pancakes and bacon." He clears his throat and places his hat on the counter beside him. "And a cup of OJ."

I laugh. "John, I'm still not a server."

He looks at me like he doesn't give a shit.

I put the mop down and say, "I'll go tell Tammy."

I'm back to mopping when John, putting away his cell phone, says, "Did you want me to finish that story?" I've actually never seen John with a cell phone. Usually he just sits at the counter eating, talking to strangers, or reading the paper. I would imagine that, being on the road, one would always want to be communicating with family somewhere. But maybe he doesn't have many people in his life. There's really only two people I'd even talk to if I went away. And one is a new friend and the other is in the hospital.

"Yeah, I totally do. And sorry about last time."

John shrugs. "You had customers to take care of."

I frown. "No excuse. And you're a customer too."

"Well, anyway, where was I?"

After thinking for a second, I say, "You were—"

He waves me off. "I'll just start over sos I can get a good rhythm going." So he talks about driving on the high mountain pass again, and the Corvette in front of him that flips. He sees this one guy—the driver—get thrown. The other guy is trapped beneath the overturned car. John was yanking on the door before realizing that it was stuck. "I would've known that, had I stopped to think for a second, but adrenaline and all that. Sos I went to break the window. I yelled at the guy to stay calm. And as I did, I realized that I saw this guy before—only a few hours before. At a diner. Much like this one." John takes a second to look around the room. "Yeah, much like this one. The guy is bloody, and glass is lodged into his face, but he's not unconscious or anything. He looks at me and gets scared, as if I'm the devil or something. He tries to escape from me, but of course he can't. I tell him again to stay calm and—"

Tammy walks up and pours John a refill on coffee. "Food'll be right out, John."

He nods.

I'm done mopping, but I don't want to leave John while he's telling the story this time. I'm holding the mop, and Tammy glances at me with some contempt. She puts the coffeepot back on the warming pad and goes to another customer.

"What crawled up her ass?" asks John.

I shrug. "No idea."

"Anyway, so I take a rock and smash the window. I pull him out, but he's fighting me. He keeps shouting, 'Get away from me! Get off me!' But the thing that struck me was how we all have the same blood. We all have the same emotions, more or less. Fear of death. Fear of pain. Sos I go searching for the other one, and he's lying facedown, and I rush over and turn him, and it's not lookin' good for him."

John wipes his eyes.

"Order up!" calls the cook, and I know it's John's order. But I can't grab his plate, or Tammy will think that I'm trying to steal her tip.

"That's one sad story, John." But I don't know why he's telling me. I don't get the relevance it has. "How long ago?"

"Oh, ten years ago now. I just couldn't get over how their blood was . . . just like mine."

"Red?"

John looks at me like I'm stupid.

"Here's the kicker—at the diner they were sitting next to each other. They were a couple . . . homosexuals. And I was so disgusted by them. I even chewed them out. Told them to get right with Jesus before it was too late.

"A few hours later they were . . . And I was trying to save . . . And I will wish till the day I die that I wasn't an asshole to those two boys. They were boys, Charlie. Probably no older than twenty-five." He pauses. "My idea of God changed that day. God changed. And he will never be the same."

Tammy puts the plate of pancakes and the plate of eggs and bacon in front of John. "Anything else?" she asks.

John says, "Just be kind to people."

Tammy looks at him, dumbfounded for a second, and then she trudges off to the kitchen, irritated.

# QUICK FALL

· · · · ·

I get home tired and stinky from work, and the TV, as usual when my dad's home, is emitting a blue light. Alcohol is wafting off him, since he was probably at the bar most of the night.

"I'm home," I say.

My dad doesn't respond, and I head up to my room. I almost don't even notice that my door is wide open. My heart lurches and my eyes go wide. "Where is he?" I bolt down the stairs and into the front room and stand right in front of the TV. "Where is Tickles?"

"Did you think I wouldn't find out? And watch your tone with me, young man."

"What did you do with him?"

I run to the door and hear, "Don't you dare leave this house. The mechanical dog is fine."

But I'm not listening to my dad. I call out, "Tickles!" It's so dark that I can't see anything in Geoffrey's yard. I have my phone and turn on the flashlight. "Tickles!" I yell again.

I hear my dad yell "Charlie!" as I dart out of the house.

In the middle of Geoffrey's yard, I stop running and yell again, "Tickles!"

From the blackness I hear a little bell, faint in the distance.

"Tickles!" I yell again.

The bell grows louder, and I hear a little yelp. I see Tickles emerge from the darkness beyond my flashlight.

He runs up to me, and I kneel down and pet him. "Oh, Tickles. So good to see you. You're a good dog. Such a good dog." I stand up. "Come on. Let's go into your real house. Away from the monster that is my dad."

Geoffrey gave me a key to the front door, in case I run out of dog food or need anything for Tickles. I unlock the door and turn around, and Tickles barks. He's stuck at the first stair. I realize that his fake leg makes it impossible for him to climb stairs. Maybe that's why Geoffrey put in a ramp at the back of his house. I assumed it was for Geoffrey, but maybe he did it for Tickles?

I go down the stairs and pick up Tickles. "And don't listen to my dad. You are not mechanical. You're the real deal, buddy." I put him down, and he runs into the kitchen, his little legs going.

The smell in Geoffrey's house is no longer sour and gag-inducing. It's actually pleasant. Lemon. Judy must still be coming over to clean while Geoffrey's in the hospital.

I check to see that Tickles has food and water, and then I am on my way out when I say, "I'll check on you tomorrow morning." I'm starting to close the door, when I look at my house and see that damn blue light emanating from the front room, and the shadow of my dad up and moving.

I stop myself from closing the door and instead go back into Geoffrey's house. "Never mind," I say to Tickles. "I think I'll stay with you tonight."

I'm making myself comfortable on Geoffrey's recliner. Tickles is next to me on the ground. "This is nice, right, buddy?"

Tickles looks at me with big brown eyes. His tail wags on the ground.

I adjust myself. It's not the most comfy chair in the world.

"This is better than seeing my dad. He isn't even giving a good reason for not letting you stay with us."

I close my eyes, though I think about how I'm still in my stinky work clothes. I also am thinking about how I'm no longer on the second floor with a fairly unobstructed view, so I'm not sure I'll be able to see or hear a UFO if one comes tonight, and that's worrying me.

I think about John's story and how emotional he was getting from something that happened a decade ago. I could picture the scene as he was telling it. I don't want to be someone who regrets something that large.

That large . . .

bits of . . .

the wreckage . . . the red blood . . .

My ear hurts as I'm lifted to my feet before I even know what's happening. My eyes are barely open. "You're coming home this minute," says my dad.

I fell asleep.

Tickles yaps and yaps, and growls, but stays a few safe feet back.

"Oww." My dad's still pulling at my ear.

He lets go, and I straighten up. We head outside, and before the door closes, I whisper, "I'll come back for you."

The moon is out, and bright, and I don't want to talk to my dad. We trot past barren grass and rocks, from one small house to another.

We get inside, and he says, "Get to bed. And if you decide to sneak out tonight, don't bother coming home."

I'm tired enough, so I don't. Even though that's all I want to do.

# RISK IT AGAIN

•••••

It's been a few days since I've seen Grandma. I feel bad about it, but I didn't forget about her, and that matters to me.

I take Tickles with me to see her. I think Tickles would prefer the company to being alone, and I'm sure my grandma would enjoy the dog.

One other thing I remember to bring is a certain picture given to me. It's black and white, and I think it's perfect for my grandma's room, so I framed it. Not only is it a great shot of the both of us, but maybe she won't forget herself, or me, as quickly?

As Tickles and I walk through the halls of the nursing home, we are stopped by 98 percent of the residents and staff. The only person who doesn't stop us to pet Tickles or remark on his leg is an older guy in a wheelchair with his head leaning to the left and his mouth wide open, snoring.

We're almost to my grandma's room when I see Susan

at the end of the hall. It has felt like months since I last saw her. And it makes me think of Seth all over again. When she sees me, she smiles and calls out my name. She walks toward me as she pushes an old lady in a wheelchair.

Her smile seems to grow bigger the closer she walks. Mine does too.

"Charlie, how are you doing? And who's this little guy?"

"I'm dog-watching for a few days. His name is Tickles."

"I'd love to pet him, but I'm allergic to dogs, sadly."

"Oh yeah. Seth said that. I should get him away from you."

Susan smiles. "It's good to see you. Seth is having fun in Seattle, but I think he misses you. At least that's my impression."

I don't know what to say to that. I miss him too. "When does he get back?"

"Two weeks."

That sounds like forever. I think my face shows my disappointment, because she says, "It'll go by quickly. He'll be back before you know it. Well, I better get Becky to her room. What's the picture?"

"Seth took it. Isn't it amazing?" I show it to her.

Susan smiles, but there's a hint of sadness in her eyes, and I wonder why. "You two are beautiful together."

I walk to my grandma's room wondering if Susan meant me and my grandma or me and Seth. And I wonder why I think that.

I knock on the doorframe to my grandma's room and walk in. She is sitting in her regular old recliner, her hands fidgety, as usual. "Hello, Grandma." She turns to me and smiles upon seeing the dog.

Tickles doesn't run up to my grandma but instead holds back behind my legs. "His name is Tickles." I turn behind me. "Tickles, what's wrong?" He doesn't seem to want to see Grandma. I finally have to pick him up, and as he shivers in my arms, I bring him to my grandma so that she can pet him.

She smiles, not noticing that the dog doesn't really want to be petted.

After a few pets, Tickles yaps.

My grandma jumps. Her face looks frightened, and I can't help but think of her reaction as that of a child who hasn't acquired words to express herself yet. Except, unlike a child, my grandma has lived a lifetime.

I put Tickles down, and he runs behind my leg again. I go to the blinds and open them. "Why do they never open these?" I ask her.

I describe the sky (*Smooth Sailing on a Glassy Sea*) and set her clock to the right time.

I grab the picture I set on her bed and hold it up to her. "Look at this. It was taken by my best friend. You remember Seth? He went on that walk with us. Where should we put it?" I look around the room, and I see she's staring intently at the picture. I point to her. "That's you. Eloise Dickens."

She is no longer smiling.

"And that's me." I point at myself in the picture. "Charlie. Your grandson. Remember me, Grandma?"

# IF THE WORLD DOESN'T WAIT, DON'T STOP

. . . . .

I can hear the beeps of the monitors down the otherwise empty, sterile hall. Whitehall's hospital is small, just one long hallway with only a few people ever inside. I bring Tickles to see Geoffrey, which I think will cheer them both up. When we get to his room, Geoffrey turns to me, his massive body covered by a white sheet. He has tubes hooked up to various parts of his body, which surprises me, but I pretend like nothing's wrong.

"Charlie," he says. "Oh, and Tickles." He smiles at us both.

Tickles can't jump up onto the bed, so he sits down next to it. I am about to pick up Tickles, but Geoffrey tells me not to put him on the bed.

I am glad to see Geoffrey, and relieved to see him alive. It's an odd thought that I think he could die. He's not even that old, but I still worry about him.

"So, what's wrong with you?" I ask.

Geoffrey chuckles a little and coughs. "Infection. They have me on some antibiotics."

"Oh." I stand there.

Geoffrey lies there.

Machines occasionally beep.

I sit in a chair. Tickles lies underneath me.

The light in the room goes from brighter to darker to brighter over the course of a few minutes. A flurry of clouds rush through the sky, hurrying to get somewhere.

Geoffrey stares up at the ceiling before turning to me. "Why don't you and I talk? You have time for that?"

I make a show of looking at my nonexistent watch. "I think I can fit you in."

Geoffrey doesn't seem to hear that comment, or if he does, he ignores it. "I've been doing a bit of thinking. Reflecting." He brings up his ex-wife. She left him for someone else. But she recently stopped by his house, even though she's living in Helena. Geoffrey could see her as she walked up the stairs to the front door. He didn't move off the green couch to answer the door. It had been many years since they'd last seen each other, and Geoffrey didn't want his ex-wife to see him at his current size.

"When was all this?" I ask.

"The marriage?" he asks.

"No. Her knocking on your door."

"About two weeks ago."

A nurse with a clipboard walks into the room to check something, and she looks at me and the dog. "No dogs allowed in the hospital. Don't you know he has an infection?"

I stand, almost as an automatic response. "Oh. Sorry." I definitely don't want to make Geoffrey worse.

"It's okay," Geoffrey says. "He's my dog."

The nurse shakes her head. "Still no dogs allowed in the hospital." She leaves the room, and Geoffrey tells me to sit.

He says, "I'd rather die with company than survive alone."

# HIDDEN

. . . . .

Tickles is curled up in a ball on his pillow bed in my room. "He can secretly stay in my room. And when I leave, I'll put him in Geoffrey's house."

"Secretly, huh?" says Seth on the other end of the line.

I lie on my bed with the world's largest smile on my face. Seth called a few minutes ago. It's the first real, uninterrupted talk we've had since he left. "But enough about my problems. How's Seattle?"

"Seattle is great. I am forgetting that I have to live in a town of three thousand people for a while."

"Are you getting good pictures?"

"Not really. Nothing amazing yet. And my dad is being a pain. But he's back at work now, so I have some more time to do my own thing."

I want to tell him I can't wait to have him back in Whitehall, but I don't know if that's cool to say. It might come off as pathetic. So I don't say anything.

"Are you there?" he asks.

"Sorry, yeah."

He chuckles. "Anyway, I better go clean up the kitchen before my dad gets home. It pisses him off when I leave plates and glasses out."

My stomach drops at the thought of going another two weeks without Seth.

"But feel free to text or call me anytime, Charlie. If you want."

"Okay," I say. "I will."

After I hang up, I notice Tickles still asleep, and I wonder if I can just sleep the next two weeks away.

# COME AS YOU ARE, LEAVE CHANGED

•••••

The sound of the balls hitting the pins ricochets around the cavernous, dim hall. I can't believe I'm at the bowling alley with my dad and his friends. I sit in front, near the lane, alone, and my dad and his buddies are in the back with beer.

One of his friends, a guy named George Smithers, just finished bowling and is walking back, passing me. "Charlie, I haven't seen you in forever. You've gotten so big. Come sit with us."

I think it's funny when people say I've gotten big, which is really the only thing adults know how to say to teenagers they haven't seen in a while, because I haven't grown much at all in a few years. I am easily one of the shortest freshmen. Or, sophomore now, I guess. Add that to the reasons why I'm picked on.

George Smithers is a tall man, and he looks at me. "Come on. Come chat."

They all make room for me as I awkwardly nudge into

the guys surrounding the table. "Charlie," laughs Ted. "Twice in a few days. What gives?"

A lot of the guys echo my name and say hi.

"I actually got him to join us tonight," says my dad. He tips a beer toward me when he says that.

I can't believe I'm joining him, because I feel like this is hell. But I don't want to disappoint my dad.

"My boy is coming too. I'm sure you know him," says a guy named Melvin.

"Who's that?" I ask.

"You know Trey Boxer," says my dad.

Images of Psych of the Ass Trio flood my mind. I didn't know Psych was Melvin's son. Oh god. I don't want to see any member of the Ass Trio tonight. Or basically ever.

George sips his beer and asks me, "Any girl in the picture?"

My face turns red. I think about Jennifer Bennett, but she's not really in the picture. At least not in the sense that George means. "Uh." I shake my head.

It's my turn to bowl, so I get up and the guys cheer me on. I take aim and hit three pins. I'm awful at bowling, and I can't wait to get home and hug Tickles. I don't talk to anyone as I wait for my ball to return. I focus on the remaining seven pins. I manage to knock four more pins down, for a total of seven pins in that frame.

"Not too bad," says Ted as he gets up to bowl.

Strike.

The guys cheer. But I sit there awkwardly, unsure what to do as I see everyone high-fiving, laughing, smiling. My fingers fidget. I twist my foot on the ground.

Ted walks back and asks what I want to do with myself

after school, as the rest of the guys cheer on another guy I don't know. By the way, this is the second-most-common thing that adults say to me, after "You've gotten big."

"Uh, not sure."

"Any job or career thoughts? Work at the mine with the rest of us?"

"Hopefully not." I immediately regret saying that, thinking I pissed off Ted. But he just laughs.

"Don't blame you."

I really have no idea what I want to do as a career. I guess I never thought I'd be on earth long enough to have to come up with one. Just then in walks Trey Boxer, aka Psych. He carries his own bowling ball in a bag at his side.

I want to sink into the chair and disappear. But I'm with my dad. And Psych isn't with the other two members of the Ass Trio. So we're evenly matched.

He sees me, glares, and mouths "Fuck you" before smiling and loudly saying, "Charlie, I didn't know you bowled." His voice is friendly and upbeat. His acting is pissing me off. But he wants the other guys to think he's something he isn't—a decent person.

"I don't." I have nothing else to say to him.

He whispers "Watch your ass" as he walks over to his own lane and puts his ball into the ball-return. What a weird thing to say, but I pretend like I don't hear him.

I watch him get a strike on his first roll. Followed by another one. And another one. And holy shit, Psych is a good bowler and not just an asshole. Though, he's still mostly an asshole. We're the only two people down on the lanes—minus the other guys who are coming and going as they bowl.

"Charlie," he says after his third strike. "You know why I bowl so well?"

I shake my head.

"I picture your face on every one of the pins." He laughs.

I stand up to bowl. "You're an asshole."

"Oh, don't get your lady panties in a bunch."

I shake my head and focus on the pins in front of me. I try picturing Psych's face on the pins, but it doesn't work. I roll a gutter ball. I hear Psych laughing in the background. Some of the guys say, "Don't worry, Charlie." Or, "You'll get 'em, Charlie."

I focus again—Psych's face on the pins. I throw the ball and get all the pins. "Strike!" I yell.

"It's a spare, you idiot," says Psych.

My dad isn't even around. Didn't even see what I did.

When Psych's up next, he passes me and says, "This time I'll picture your boyfriend's face on the pins."

He stands facing the pins, his bowling ball in hand. Anger has built in my chest, and as he starts to swing, I run up to him and push him from behind. The ball flies off his fingers and slams into the lane before rolling right into the gutter. Psych falls to the floor and slides. But he's not hurt. Damn. I fucked up his game, though, which counts as a win to me.

Before I know it, Psych is up and trying to punch my stomach. I'm holding on to him so he can't pull his arm back enough to do real damage. The adults run over and separate us.

"Charlie," says my dad, taking hold of my shoulders. "What the hell is going on?"

Psych's dad is asking the same thing of his son.

I shake my head. "Nothing."

Psych says the same thing.

"Apologize to Trey," says my dad. "For pushing him."

I look at Psych. He mouths "Fuck you" again. I shake my head.

"Charlie," says my dad more sternly.

"No."

"Okay, come on," says my dad as he pulls me by the arm. "I think you've had enough bowling."

I gotta get out of here. Everything seems too surreal. He pulls me to the hallway near the bathroom and says, "What has gotten into you?"

"He's a dick, Dad. Psych—Trey—is a bully."

"Oh, come on now, Charlie. You're being dramatic. Besides, you shoved him."

"Yeah, and he deserves worse."

"I think you'd better go home."

"Fine. I never wanted to go bowling anyway. It's stupid."

My dad sighs. "And no UFOs tonight. Promise me."

I stand there.

"Don't test me right now, Son."

"Fine."

"You'd better be home when I get there."

"Yeah? And when will that be?" I don't say that. I want to, but he's already heading back to the guys and Psych is smirking at me, and this whole night is stupid.

I'm heading home like I promised my dad. But nothing was said about not taking my sweet time and walking the slowest, longest path possible, all the while occasionally looking up into the Great Beyond.

I'm still pissed about Psych. I really wish I could've beaten the shit out of him. Though, I probably would've lost.

But I'm also pissed at my dad. He brushed it all off—and worse, made me feel like it was all my fault. Was it? Was I the one in the wrong?

This is one of those nights when my heart feels empty but my chest feels heavy and the world feels upside down. This is one of those nights when I'd like aliens to come save me.

# FIRE ALARM

·····

I have one of those rare summer day shifts, so I'm biking to work wearing my black pants and black shirt. Except I'm melting in the suddenly-turned 100-degree day. Every second on my bike is like riding through a furnace. I will be a sweaty mess when I get to work. I can't wait to own an air-conditioned truck.

Larry the manager mostly works during the days, and greets me with, "Glad you could join us for your shift."

My shift starts in three minutes, and I've already clocked in. So I'm not sure what Larry is complaining about, and I don't really care.

"Who works today?" I ask.

"Tammy. And she's having 'Billy trouble,' so don't get in her way. Made that mistake last night." He clenches his jaw.

The afternoon shift manages to stay fairly busy. I hate being a busboy, and I keep trying to nudge my way into serving, but apparently there's not a huge need for new servers.

"Don't forget," Larry says as he passes me with a sand-wich and fries, "checks are in the office."

"Oh, right. I'd love to get mine."

"Give me a minute. Jesus."

"I mean, when you have a chance." My face is beet red.

Larry calls me back to his paper-filled office a few min-utes later and hands me an envelope with my name on it. "There. Now you can go buy yourself whatever stupid video game is popular right now." For being barely thirty, Larry is one bitter man. I wonder if he has a girlfriend.

"Larry?"

"What?" he asks as he looks at the top paper in a stack on his desk.

"Uh. Can I go on break?"

"Yeah, yeah. Go."

I go to the hallway and hang up my apron. I open my envelope and see that I have a check for eighty-nine dollars. I'm rich! I smile as I go to the convenience store next door.

Scanning the bookrack, I don't see the book I'm dying to have. I keep looking and swoop back for another attack. I move some books to the side and finally spot it. Thank god. I look around, making sure no one is watching me grab the store's only copy of *Montana UFO Sightings*.

I try to hide my smile, but it's hard.

I find myself back in the staff cubby space, with the time clock and some boxes to put belongings in. I'm reading the last of the book's introduction before my break ends, and Larry walks in. "Whatcha got there?" He grabs the book out of my hands.

"Um."

"*Montana UFO Sightings*, huh? Didn't know you were into that sort of shit."

"I'm—"

"Nut jobs, every single one of 'em."

Luckily, Larry isn't a Whitehall native and wasn't here to know the story of my mom's fall from grace. But I need to keep a low profile and keep from being seen in public with this book again—because if a Whitehall native sees me, well, not only would my dad be furious, but my life would get worse, which scares me, because I'm not sure how that's possible.

Larry laughs. "You're a weird kid, dude." He shoves the book into my chest and walks off, laughing.

I let out a big breath, and quickly hide the book.

# DÉJÀ VU (IF ONLY)

.....

I'm biking home from my afternoon shift. It's about seven p.m. and still super hot out. When I get to the main street, I spot Jennifer Bennett halfway down the block with a couple of friends. They're in a small line on the sidewalk to buy tickets to the movie. I'm hoping that she has forgotten all about when she saved me from the Ass Trio.

This is my chance. I could push through most of the steps of Mission Probably Improbable. I could play coy, go into the theater, and when they're buying popcorn, I'd see them and be like, "Oh! Hey, girls. I didn't know you were here." They'd all look at one another with smiles on their faces, and then Jennifer would ask me to sit with them. We'd share popcorn and soda and laugh and cry, and I'd end the night with a kiss from Jennifer Bennett, my new girlfriend, because she'd realize how adorable and funny I am.

I don't think she has actually seen me, as I'm pedaling slowly and am still fifty or so feet away. And I realize that (a) I stink like fryers and fried food and bleach, (b) I look gross from the heat of biking both to and from work, and, most important, (c) I am holding a book that no one should see me carrying, for various historical and contemporary reasons.

The girls are laughing as they head into the theater through the open doors.

I look at the old marquee to see what they're going to watch. It's a movie called *Cain* and is supposedly one of the biggest hits of the summer. Though, we got it two months after it was initially released across the country. We get all our movies late—if we get them at all.

When I reach the front of the theater, I stop riding.

I linger, seriously contemplating buying a ticket, before realizing how stupid an idea it is. Even if I saw them inside, they wouldn't talk to me. If anything, Jennifer would feel more sorry for me sitting alone. I can't date someone who pities me. I shake my head as I get onto my bike and pedal home, hoping that no one sees me.

# SILENCE CAN ECHO LOUDLY

•••••

The sun is setting and the sky is growing dark, and my dad has yet to come home. Tickles is splayed out on the floor, alternating between asleep and moaning, and awake and panting. Since we're on the second floor, it's boiling, and my shirt has stuck to my sweating body.

I'm looking out my window and taking a break from my *Montana UFO Sightings* book. "Tickles, this is a fascinating sunset. I'd call it, uh, *Colored Coals Below the Surface*. It's all these red, orange, and fiery colors bubbling out from the horizon."

Tickles doesn't even raise his head. I look back at my bed and how I'm almost done reading my new book, and I think how I could also just be leaving the movie theater with my new girlfriend, if only I had had the guts to go in.

I bend over, pick Tickles up, and place him on the bed with me. He looks groggy and tired, walks in a circle once, and then moves to the edge of the bed and kind of slides off and sits back down on the floor. So much for cuddling with the dog.

Back on my bed, I pick up the book, which was left open on the bedsheets. "Tickles, some of the sightings are fascinating.

"For instance, a guy in Butte once saw seven discs hover above a dormant volcano. This is what he said. 'I was walking my dog, when out of nowhere Sam starts barking, and I look up and see these seven flat, saucer-like discs hovering above the *M*.' That's what they call the volcano mountain because it has a big *M* made of white rocks on it. 'The whole event lasted about ten seconds, but I was able to take a picture. Only one before they all vanished. They didn't even fly away. It was almost like they just became invisible. Sam looks up at the mountain every time we go for our walks now.'

"What do you think of that? What would you do if you saw a UFO? Huh, buddy?" I'm not looking at Tickles, for fear that he's sleeping and I'll feel like a big idiot. "The picture is included. You want to see it?" Tickles doesn't say anything, so I just study it. Sure enough, seven creepy thin discs are hovering around this lone mountain peak on the edge of Butte.

The silence in the room builds, and the darkness grows as the daylight dims, but the small nightstand light is doing its best to keep me in a cone of ember light.

Tickles is snoring now and occasionally flicking his back leg, and I'm thankful for his company. I flip back to the table of contents to find another story I liked. "Oh yeah, Tickles. This is a good one.

"There was this school yard in Helena, Montana.

This was about ten years ago. The kids were at recess with some teachers when what appeared to be an orb on fire flew right above them and landed with a crash not too far away. They show pictures of the crash site in the book, but the report says there was nothing at the site but some liquid ooze on the ground and busted-up trees. They called officials, who went to the site. The officials weren't sure what it was, but it wasn't a meteor, because there were no fragmentary space rocks left behind. Whatever crash-landed either disintegrated or up and left. Isn't that crazy? But don't you see? This is all validation for my own search. My mom's right, we're not alone."

Tickles's snoring has gotten louder, and I can't bring myself to keep talking to a sleeping dog. But I'm not alone as the darkness finishes taking over the daylight.

I go for a walk because I am hot and sweaty and want to escape the hot box that is my bedroom. Tickles was sleeping away, and I said, "Walk?" But he didn't even lift his head. I said it again, but the only thing he did was flick his ear in a way that I interpreted as, *Leave me alone.* So I figured the little guy needed his sleep.

The street seems abandoned as I leave my house. I look at Geoffrey's house and notice that it now appears stagnant, which isn't the case when he's home. The only thing that feels alive to me at this moment is the sky.

I walk up the dirt road to the forest. The same one I always bring Tickles on. But the silence is just too thick tonight. I want to call Seth because I haven't heard from him in a while, but I am hoping he'll call me so that I don't have to bother him on vacation. Even though I know it's my turn.

It's almost ten in Montana, so it's almost nine in Seattle. I figure that's a decent time to call. I know we're friends, but even still, I can't quite convince myself that I'm not being an intruder on Seth's time. But I'm also conflicted, because I suspect he's feeling the same way.

Ugh.

"Just dial," I tell myself. My palms feel sticky, and it's not because of the lingering heat.

Maybe tonight will be the night the UFO reappears? If so, I shouldn't be distracting myself with a phone call. I'll call him later.

After about twenty minutes I find myself on the rock I fell asleep on.

I stand on top of the rock and look all around the quiet forest. I have a sudden urge to yell and let my lungs expand. But I don't know what to yell. But the urge is still there, so I yell out, "Ahhhhhhhhh!"

After I stop, the quiet quickly settles back in. I stare up at the stars, and suddenly I have a whole bunch to say. So I say it all, but I don't yell it. I just whisper it. Sometimes I feel like the universe hears a whisper more loudly than a yell. "Where are you? I hope you're safe. I hope you're happy. I hope you come back for me. I'm waiting for the day when you come back. You know where to find me. . . . And I still want to know why."

I stare up at the big black sky and see the tiny stars twinkle, and I wait.

And wait.

The blackness above echoes back at me. Expanding. I

feel like my words are coming back at me—as if they don't have anywhere else to go. As if there's no one up there to hear them. As if my mom isn't up there at all.

Without really thinking about it, I pull out my phone and call.

"Charlie!" he answers.

I feel so confused that I suddenly want to cry. Seth answered my call. But why did I ever think he wouldn't?

"Charlie? Hello? You there?"

Not sure what's going on in my mind at the moment, but I'm caught in a swirl of thoughts.

"I'm hanging up unless you say something," says Seth.

"Hi," I manage to say.

"There you are." He laughs. "I'm so glad you called."

"You are?" I ask, surprised. I sit on the rock. "So how's your trip?"

The blackness of the sky is less overwhelming. The tiny stars shine a little more brightly. Interesting how sometimes all it takes is a hello to break the feeling of insignificance.

# TAKE IT BACK

·····

I talk with Seth for a long time on the rock and for most of
the walk home. He talks about Seattle and his dad and the
pictures he's taking, and I mostly just listen. I decide that
I like listening to Seth. I don't need to say anything to be
content. He could talk forever, and I'd be happy with that.

For the first time in a long time it appears as if my
house is alive. There's a light on, which means one thing.

"Uh-oh. I gotta go. I'll talk to you tomorrow."

"Everything okay?"

"Yeah. I hope so."

"Charlie?"

"Yeah?"

"Call me if anything's wrong, okay? Promise me."

"I will. Bye, Seth." I run up the walkway and into the
house.

Yep, I know something's up when it's nearly eleven and
my dad isn't watching the TV. He's in the kitchen slam-
ming cupboards when I enter.

"Where were you?" he demands. He seems unsteady in his movements and wobbly when he stands there.

"The forest."

"The forest?" he mocks. "Looking for damn UFOs, I suppose."

"Why aren't you watching TV?" I ask.

A rage blooms in his eyes. "Did you think I wouldn't find out again? You are—I don't even know—in trouble."

"About me going to into the woods?"

"About that damn dog."

"Tickles?" My heart sinks because I left him in my room. But I know my dad won't reason with me. He's in the mood where if you try to reason with him, he'll explode in anger.

"I don't even know what to do with you anymore. You are purposely disrespecting me."

"I was going to take him back before you got home."

"Oh." He forces a laugh. "That makes it okay?"

I don't say anything. The smell of alcohol is particularly strong tonight.

"Huh?" He flashes in anger.

"No, sir," I say softly.

"Damn right."

"It's just—" I shouldn't say any more, but now I've drawn attention to it.

"What, boy? What?"

"Lonely. Is all. He's, uh, in that house all by himself. I can keep him company until Geoffrey gets back from the hospital."

My dad looks at me. He fills a cup of water from the faucet and takes a sip. "I see your mother in you. And it's not good. I'm doing my best to get rid of that, for your sake, but you always fighting me on everything doesn't make it any easier for either of us."

I feel so far from my father at this moment. He's so foreign. So alien. How could anyone love this man when he talks so terribly about the people he supposedly loves?

My dad sits down at the table.

"Why can't he just stay here? It'd be so much easier."

My dad sits, he rubs his eyes. "You're boneheaded, just like your mother. Your crazy mother. You know this, right, Charlie?"

"Don't say that," I say under my breath.

"Speak up," he says.

"Don't say that!" I scream.

My dad stares into my eyes. "Don't be so melodramatic. Although, that's another trait you must've gotten from her."

"She's helping humanity! She's with the aliens, and they're coming back for me and not you! They don't want you!"

"Charlie, listen—"

"You're worthless to them! To me! To everyone!" I run up to my room and slam the door as hard as I ever have.

The walls shake slightly, and in a weird way that feels good. For the first time in a long while the house is very much alive.

# THE IDEA HATCHES

·····

I'm sitting on her bed, watching Grandma twist her thumbs around each other. The heat wave has been continuing. It's only the last week of June, and we've already had five straight days of 100 degrees. I leave Grandma's blinds down today so that it can stay somewhat cool in her cave.

Her clock is two minutes behind today. "Can't your clock make up its mind?" I ask my grandma. But she's in a different mood when the blinds are drawn. She's not exactly more morose, but more subdued, which is kind of hard to picture, since she doesn't do much as it is.

The air ducts in the nursing home rattle, and cool air starts flowing into the cave. I hear a collective sigh throughout the building.

Her house was built by my grandpa, Harold, when he was a young man. He died in that house. She stayed until she could stay no longer. The floor plan was simple but functional. The kitchen was large—designed for when people spent a lot of time cooking, cleaning, and having meals together. At least that's what my grandma said.

She lived only four blocks away. She used to be my babysitter when my dad was at work and my mom was unable to care for me.

I was standing on a footstool, and my grandma leaned over my shoulder. "Okay. Take this roller and push down and roll out like this. Then do that to each side."

She was making a pie and had leftover crust—homemade, not from a box—that she let me practice with. We would put some mini pies into the cupcake tray. I'd make those ones. Proudly.

She handed me the roller. Our hands and chests were covered in flour. Or at least mine were.

I pushed and rolled. I tore the crust and wanted to cry.

She smiled kindly. "Whoops. It's all right. It's just crust. Let's try again, Charlie." She grabbed it and rolled it back into a ball with some water.

I tried again and again. And I finally managed to make a flat, non-holed, mini piecrust.

"Wonderful. Okay. Now we take it and place it in the tray like this." I watched her carefully maneuver the crust into a tin tray. I tried and succeeded with my mini crust on the first try. "You're getting good at this."

My face lit up.

Susan pokes her head in and says, "Hi, Charlie. Feels like forever since I've seen you."

I have an idea about getting Grandma out of her cave for a bit.

"Hey, Susan? How is someone able to get a patient to leave for a day?"

A family member (adult) has to fill out and sign a form in order to release a patient (for up to four hours) from the retirement home, so I find myself waiting for my dad at home. He'll be happy that I'm not out chasing UFOs.

He comes in the back door, and I'm in the kitchen with my phone, texting Seth. He sent me a couple of edited pictures that he took in Seattle. I'm certain he is going to be a famous photographer one day.

"What is this?" my dad says.

I look around. "What?"

"You're in the kitchen when I get home. What did you do?"

"Nothing. But . . . I have a question." I tell him my plan, and he pops open a beer.

He interrupts me. "You should've come bowling tonight. Trey was asking about you. He's a nice boy."

I shake that nasty thought off. "Please, Dad? She needs to get out of there. Just for one day."

"Absolutely not." He takes a swig of beer and sets the can on the table.

"Why not?"

I don't understand why he doesn't want his mom around more. Or a dog. Or me, frankly.

"Because I already have plans for the Fourth of July, and they don't include taking care of a woman who won't know what's going on anyway."

"Plans?"

"Yeah, me and the guys are going fishing."

"Well, can you sign the papers, and I'll take her to watch the parade?"

My dad shakes his head. "Not a chance." He turns away from me, letting me know that the conversation is done.

I huff. "Well, can we at least have Tickles stay with us?"

"You're pushing on my last nerve, Charlie. Go do something."

I huff more loudly and stomp out of the kitchen, saying, "As long as it's a preapproved something, right?"

My dad doesn't respond. I don't even know if he really even heard me. And speaking of last nerves, his drinking is getting on mine. He always drank. From as far back as I can remember, he'd have a beer when he got home, but ever since his wife disappeared and his mother disappeared, just in a different way, he's been drinking more.

Would my dad prefer that I drink instead of search for UFOs?

# THE GREATEST HEIST
# WHITEHALL HAS EVER SEEN

· · · · ·

Whitehall has this big event for the Fourth of July. In terms of holiday festivities, this is the town's biggest. There's a parade at noon and then a barbecue right after in the park, the same one that Seth had his allergic reaction in.

Speaking of which, Seth comes home in two days. So there's that excitement. But today, July Fourth, there's going to be some sneakiness and some stealthiness and a good old-fashioned robbery.

Just kidding on that last one.

But the thought of my grandma sitting alone in that dark room today saddens me. So I decided to break her out . . . by forging my dad's signature on the release papers.

Normally I don't think that alone would work, because an adult needs to be there to actually pick up the person the nursing home is releasing. But I have fortune on my side because Susan loves me. And she would never think of me as the lying type. And I'm usually not. Except when it's for a good cause.

I show up in my grandma's room. "Surprise," I say, and she slowly looks at me and absently smiles. "I have a surprise for you today, Grandma." I walk over to her and whisper, "We're breaking you out of here."

I have the plan all figured out. The paperwork has already been given to Susan. I said my dad was just running a few last-minute errands and he'd be here soon to pick Grandma up.

Except it's already eleven thirty.

And my dad is fishing.

But I will use the noon parade as pressure. So this is how my plan works:

I put a thick layer of sunscreen on Grandma's face, then put on her sweet-looking sunglasses and a red, white, and blue hat. She's already wearing a red, white, and blue shirt. Then I get her into the wheelchair—not that she can't walk, of course, but just for getting her out of here quickly. I roll her to the front doors and stand next to her, waiting. We are both looking out as if expecting someone. She is doing it because that's what she always does. I am doing it because I want Susan to think my dad is coming. Because that's what I told her.

At 11:45 I say, "Susan, he just texted me that the parade is blocking his car from driving over to this side of town. So he's walking. I just hope he's not too late, or the whole day will be ruined."

At 11:50 I say, "I don't know where he is."

At 11:55 I wheel my decked-out grandma back to her room with the saddest expression a teenage boy could ever have. As we pass Susan at her nurse station, I say, "Never mind. He won't be here in time."

"Sorry, Charlie," says Susan, who watches me wheel Grandma back down the hall. Then, as if right on cue, she says, "Wait, Charlie. He's on his way?"

I turn and nod.

She looks at me and then at Grandma. "Why don't you just take her to your dad?"

"Oh, really?" My eyes are wide. "Thank you! Grandma will love this."

Susan bends down. "Now, Eloise, you be on your best behavior. Okay?"

Grandma doesn't respond. It's like she doesn't even realize that someone is talking to her. Or she knows exactly what she's doing and doesn't want to be on her best behavior.

# THE LOST PARADE

· · · · ·

I'm wheeling her down the sidewalk, telling her the plan, and she knows something is up, but I don't think she knows what. I tell her it's the Fourth of July parade, but she doesn't seem to register that.

We'll watch the parade, and then I'll promptly bring her back to the nursing home, and neither Susan nor my dad will be any the wiser. I won't even take Grandma to the town barbecue. I just want her to experience something other than her cave.

After ten minutes of pushing her, she tries to stand as I'm rolling the wheelchair. "No, Grandma. Stay seated."

She pushes my hands away.

"Grandma, sit." I hold my hand on her shoulder as I continue to push her.

The parade is already in progress when we get there. I find a place and park the wheelchair so that she can see without anyone standing in front of her.

I must admit that the parade is kind of lame. I mean,

it's a small town, so there's one small marching band and some people riding in cars. And some horses (it is Montana, after all).

But I'm happy because people are cheering and shaking those small American flags, and there's just a lot of excitement. I'm also pleased that I brought Grandma.

I spot Jennifer Bennett across the street. She is writing in a small notepad and occasionally looking up. I figure she is reporting on the parade for the *Whitehall Courier*.

I'm mesmerized, watching her methodically write and look up and write. Actually, I'm just mesmerized by her. She seems to work harder than any other teenager at our school. And she isn't into playing sports or cheerleading. Not that I'm against those things, but I'd have more in common with a reporter than a volleyball player.

Mission Probably Improbable: Step one—talk to her.

My phone buzzes, and it breaks the spell. Happy Fourth of July! I miss you, Charlie. I'm almost home. And then we can start our summer adventures!

I smile. I snuck my grandma out. We're at the parade. Don't tell your mom!

Putting the phone away, I turn to the wheelchair, and my grandma's gone. What? Where did she go? How did I not notice her leave?

I quickly scan the area. She couldn't have gone far, but I don't see her anywhere.

I take hold of the wheelchair, stare intently both ways, and then choose left. I doubt she headed toward the nursing home, the way we just came.

It's hard trying to maneuver an empty wheelchair around people who not only barely budge out of your way, but also throw annoyed glances at you, because who pushes an empty wheelchair at a parade?

Charlie Dickens does.

People I know say hi or ask what I'm doing, but I just keep looking for Grandma. I could get into a ton of trouble if I don't find her.

Like, a ton of trouble. My heart skips a beat just thinking about it.

"Eloise?" I shout, but the parade is so loud that no one pays any attention, and probably least of all my grandma. I shout her name again.

I'm looking all around, and I wish Seth were here to help me.

The panic inside me is growing exponentially every second that I don't spot her.

"Grandma!"

A large woman slurping a large soft drink turns and looks at me. "Who are you shouting for?"

"Have you seen an old woman pass by here? She's about five feet tall. Mostly shuffles her feet."

She shakes her head. "Sorry, kid. Let me ask Ned." She turns to the man next to her and nudges him. "Have you seen an old lady pass by here?"

The man shakes his head and turns back to the parade.

The woman looks back to me and shrugs.

I see an older guy wearing a cowboy hat farther back from the street. "Did you see an old woman pass by here?"

He ponders for a moment and then nods. I get excited, hoping that I'm close. "I can't say as I did," he finally mutters.

*Seriously, guy?* I want to ask. Why did you nod only to

say no? But instead I turn quickly and head in the other direction. I am jogging as best as I can. I feel my phone vibrate.

Shoot. I pull it out while still jogging.

My dad.

My dad never calls. Especially when on a fishing trip. Something must be up. He must know.

I am dead.

Oh god.

I put the phone back. "Eloise!" I shout.

I reach the end of the parade route and don't see her anywhere. It's almost like she has just disappeared. Just up and vanished like my mother. I wonder about the possibility of that. But I didn't see any UFO or anything out of the ordinary. But maybe that's the point. Maybe the aliens work on a level where they don't want us to see them or know of their existence. Maybe they're hiding in plain sight?

I want to cry, I'm so upset about losing my grandma.

But then I hear people shouting and I see pointing. Someone near me says, "What's she doing?"

I hear another person say, "She's stopping the parade."

My heart sinks before I even look. I follow the finger of the person pointing and see Grandma leaning into the driver's window of a car in the middle of the parade. She shuffles down to the next car, and I see people run out after her. I dart out into the parade route and shout, "Grandma." She is good at pretending not to hear me.

As I get closer to her, I realize that she's asking everyone, "Where's Harold? Have you seen Harold?"

I sigh and put my hand on her arm.

She flinches. She doesn't even know who is touching her.

"Grandma, it's me. Charlie. Your grandson."

The guy who was talking to her turns to me. "She seems like a sweet lady. She yours?"

I nod. "I need to get her back to the nursing home." I turn to her. "Grandma, sit in the wheelchair."

She doesn't like that my hand is still on her forearm, but she manages to look at me and say, "Where's Harold?"

I don't want to tell her he's dead. All I need right now is for her to sit down so that I can get her back to the nursing home. "He's home. Let's go back there." I feel like a royal jerk. Though I find solace, even if I don't fully forgive myself, in the knowledge that I'm pretty sure she will have forgotten what I said by the time we get back. I hope so, because the way her eyes light up tells me that not only does she remember her husband of forty years, but he was the light of her life.

Now I feel even worse. I'm a terrible person who is probably going to hell.

# EXPOSED

.....

I'm telling Seth about the adventure with Grandma today. I'm on my bed without my shirt, slowly cooking in the heat that is trapped in my room. The fan is on and the windows are open, since it has cooled off outside.

Oh, and I'm not taking any more chances today, so Tickles is stuck at Geoffrey's house. But I left a light on for him, with the TV on, and the window's open. He'll be good.

"Yeah, and I managed to get her back to the nursing home in one piece."

"Well, that's good. You did a crazy thing today, Charlie. It's pretty awesome, actually."

"I'm pretty sure the whole escape was pointless. I don't even think she knew a parade was happening. And she probably watched five seconds of it."

"Hey, at least she got out and experienced some life—which is what you wanted her to do."

"That's true."

The back door bangs open and closed. Some rustling of bags, and my dad yells up, "Charlie?"

"Shoot. My dad's home. I better go."

"Good luck!"

"For what?" I ask.

"Didn't you say he called?"

"Damn. I forgot to call him back, didn't I?"

Seth chuckles. "Sounds like it. Let me know how it goes."

I take a deep breath and yell down to my dad, "Yeah?"

"Get down here, young man."

I hope he hasn't heard anything. I really hope, because it's such a small town that when weird things happen, word travels at the speed of a UFO.

I remember this one time in sixth grade. I was watching TV when my dad burst into the house, pulling my mom by her shirt collar. "What the hell were you thinking?" he demanded.

She just smiled.

"Huh? The entire town heard you. The entire town!"

She closed her eyes with the smile still on her lips. It was like she was in some zone that she didn't want to leave. I was riveted by what was happening but stayed glued to the couch. I thought that once they realized I was right there, my dad would tell me to go to my room.

At school the next day, kids stared at me like I was some alien. Some laughed. Joey started that. He saw me, pointed, and laughed. "Hey, Charlie Dickens. Heard your crazy-ass mom yesterday yelling about aliens. That explains soooo much."

I didn't know exactly what she had yelled, but it was something about all of us needing to get our affairs in order. Aliens were coming to save us.

She was wrong.

Aliens had only come to save her.

My dad's face is sunburned. He wears a tank top and shorts—this is an outfit I rarely see him in. A small red cooler sits on the table.

"How was fishing?"

"What were you doing today?" He drops a knife into the sink and takes a bag of fish from the cooler.

"What do you mean?"

"You didn't answer my call or call me back."

"I was at the parade and didn't want to bug you."

My dad gives me a *Come on* look. "You need to call me back when I call you. Got it?"

"Yes."

"Good. Now, did you have dinner?" he asks.

I shake my head. "Not yet."

"Perfect, 'cause we're having trout. You can help me cook." He hands me the bag of freshly caught fish. Holding the heavy bag, I'm momentarily stunned. I can't remember the last time my dad and I cooked dinner together.

He turns back to the cooler. "Oh, and if you had called, I would've told you that I thought about it some more, and I'm fine with having that dog stay at our house."

"Wait. Really?"

He nods and turns back to face me. "But a few ground rules. You need to clean up after him. And feed him. And if he's loud or eats my shoes or clothes or anything that doesn't belong in his mouth, then he's back over there. Got it?"

This is great news.

"Maybe it'll get your mind off of aliens," he says.

My dad knows exactly how to kill any elation.

# A SMALL STORY

•••••

This time I put Tickles into a small doggie carrier and hope that no one pays much attention.

I get to Geoffrey's hospital room, peek in, and knock on the doorframe.

Geoffrey lifts his head and turns. He has a cup over his mouth for oxygen.

He pulls the mask down to his neck. "Charlie. Good to see you."

I hold up the doggie carrier.

He smiles. "And Tickles."

Tickles yaps at hearing Geoffrey say his name. I put the carrier down on the bed. "Want me to let him out?"

Geoffrey shakes his head. "Don't want to get you in trouble." He's looking a bit better and a bit worse. His cough appears to be gone, at least right now. But his skin has no color. It's like he's a ghost.

I notice he has no flowers or cards. Nothing from anyone. That makes me sad. I wonder if his mom or his ex-wife knows he's here.

"How are you feeling?" I ask.

"Fine, fine." He waves the question off with his hasty reply. This makes me think the opposite.

"How much longer are you going to be here?"

"Not sure. Hopefully not much longer. But I'm fighting a nasty infection."

I nod and look around his room. "Oh. Good news. My dad says Tickles can stay at our house until you go home."

Geoffrey smiles. "That's great news. I bet Tickles loves staying with you way more than with me." Geoffrey closes his eyes and seems to go somewhere else. As I watch him, my mind drifts—

I got home from school the day Joey laughed at me for whatever my mom had said the day before.

I did my homework, what little I had. My mom was acting weird. She was more spacey than normal. More withdrawn.

The night came, and my dad had yet to come home.

She had yet to make dinner. I honestly thought that she might've forgotten about making dinner. Or forgotten that dinner existed as a thing.

I knocked on her bedroom door, and she was standing at her bedroom window looking out to the Great Beyond.

"What's wrong, Mom?"

She turned to me, startled. She hadn't heard me enter. Or knock, apparently.

She smiled at me. "Come here, Charlie."

I walked over and stood next to her. Her room was so dark, it felt like we were both shadows.

I know now that she was becoming a shadow. A thing that, once light shone upon it, would disappear.

"What are you looking at?" I asked.

"Not looking at. But looking for."

I was curious. "For aliens?"

She turned to me and looked into my eyes. "How'd you know that?"

I felt like I was losing my mother, that she was water slipping through my fingers, and the faster I tried to grab at her, the quicker she slipped through.

"I heard about yesterday."

She turned back to the window. "They're coming for me, Charlie." She ran her hand through my hair. "I saw them the other day. They said they'd be back for me."

I looked up at her. "But I don't want you to leave."

She smiled at me like I was a naïve child. "Don't worry, sweetie. I told them about you, too. They're coming for me and you."

"What about Dad?"

She lost her smile. "Not him. Not him." She finished rubbing my hair. "Just us. We'll be together and we'll be special. And we'll be helping our species."

"How?"

She smiled. "It's complicated. But you'll see. You'll see soon. Now let's get you to bed. It's getting late."

"I'm hungry."

"Did you not eat dinner?"

I shook my head.

"Right. Dinner. Let's go make dinner."

Some time passes, and I clear my throat because I don't know whether Geoffrey has fallen asleep or has forgotten I'm here.

His eyelids pop open. "Sorry. Sorry, Charlie."

I smile.

"This hospital really has me thinking back over my life."

I think this is an odd thing to say. But I constantly think over my life. Little moments are always popping up at all kinds of random times.

"Anything you want to share?" I ask. "And does your mom know you're here? Should I contact her for you?"

Geoffrey looks at me. "She knows. Just not about . . ." He looks down at himself. "My size." He turns to me.

I want to ask him how he could get so fat. How could anyone let themselves get so fat? But I know that's rude. I know that's a truly inconsiderate thing to ask another human being.

"You're wondering how I got so fat, aren't you?" he asks.

I look like a deer caught in headlights as my heart beats heavily. I don't know what to say.

Geoffrey chuckles. "That's a yes."

I shrug. "I mean, you don't have to tell me anything. I'm not really that curious."

Geoffrey closes his eyes again. "I wanted to be big," he says.

What? I don't know if I heard him correctly.

"At first. I wanted to be a big guy because all my life I was so skinny. 'Skin and bones' everyone used to say. And I was. I was six feet tall but only a hundred and thirty pounds. In group pictures I would practically be invisible."

He holds the oxygen mask up to his mouth and breathes deeply.

"So I think I had just graduated from college and started my first job, and I was so nice to people, and I just remember everyone taking advantage of me. I don't know. Something about how easily people just walked all over me. I felt like I wasn't intimidating or worth caring about."

"So you decided to get fat?"

"I'm getting to it," he says, annoyed.

"Sorry."

"So I decided to lift weights. Be healthy, right?"

I nod.

"And it worked, kind of. But I wasn't really gaining a lot of muscle. At least not quickly. So I read all those muscle magazines, and they told me to eat more. Eat a ton. I started eating all day every day and going to the gym. It worked in the sense that I was gaining muscle quickly, but I also started gaining fat, too."

I seriously can't believe what Geoffrey is telling me. Or that he is being so forthcoming with all this.

"At first I was freaking out about being fat. But it quickly became apparent that I could gain fat a lot faster than I could gain muscle. And really the end result was comparable. I just wanted to be bigger. So I stopped going to the gym and gained more and more fat. Well, my wife at the time . . ." He looks at me and says, "I married young." And then he goes back to this other place in his mind. "She was growing more concerned with my expanding waistline. So I stopped getting fat. But I was about two hundred and fifty pounds. I had gained over a hundred and twenty pounds of muscle and fat and no longer felt invisible.

"My wife wanted me to lose the fat, obviously. But I

couldn't bring myself to do that. It'd be like losing myself again. But I decided to stop gaining weight. Well, another year or so went by, and I noticed that my clothes were tighter. I stepped on the scale, and it said two hundred seventy. I was only twenty-eight years old and was already two hundred and seventy pounds. It was like my body wasn't stopping even though I was no longer consciously trying to gain weight.

"My wife eventually left me, not because of my waist but because we weren't working, or so she said. I still felt so invisible, you know? So I just ate. And ate. Not because I wanted to get fatter. I didn't. But I was just so hungry that I couldn't stop eating. And ten years later, here I am. As hungry as ever. But not able to do anything about it."

Tears form in Geoffrey's eyes. "I can't believe I did this to myself. Now I can't even move without help." The tears are streaking his wide cheeks.

I feel sorry for Geoffrey. I don't know what to say. I don't know what to do. Tickles yelps. He wants out of that doggie carrier.

I stand, and realize that Geoffrey should be happy for at least one thing. He got what he wanted, because now everyone who looks at him can't look away. And yet he still comes across as a small person. You know?

I wish I could do something to help him.

# COME WITH ME

.....

I hold a puzzle in my hand as I walk through the nursing home. I figure Grandma can do something in here besides twiddle her fingers. The parade plan I had was a disaster.

I don't see Susan at the nurse's station. I am almost to my grandma's room when I hear her voice behind me. "Hi, Charlie."

I turn and smile. "Hi, Susan."

"You probably know that Seth gets back tomorrow."

The thought has barely let me think about anything else lately. I am so happy that my best friend comes back tomorrow. I nod.

"I know he's been missing you. So I was wondering, Do you want to go pick him up at the airport with me in Butte tomorrow night? It'd be kind of like a surprise. He'd love it."

My heart jumps at the idea. "Totally! Yes! I'd love to." I backpedal because I came off as too excited. "Yeah, that would be cool."

Susan smiles. "Great. Now shhh. Don't tell him. Let's make it a big surprise."

I can't wipe the smile off my face. I am going to surprise Seth tomorrow night. And then we'll begin our summer adventures together.

Finally.

"One other thing," she says. "I'll let Dr. Book know you're here. He wants to talk to you about Eloise."

My forehead creases. "Something wrong?"

Susan walks toward me and in a hushed voice says, "She's wet the bed twice this week. I think the doctor is planning on having her wear Depends."

"Adult diapers," I say.

Has it come to this?

# THE PLANE HAS ARRIVED

·····

I pace around the Butte airport baggage claim waiting for Seth's plane to arrive. The place feels sterile, almost like a nursing home. And I don't think that's because of Susan. She is standing there patiently.

"Charlie, calm down. What are you so nervous for?"

"Not nervous."

Truth is, I'm freaking out. Seth is moments away from seeing me, and I am moments away from seeing him. Even though it's been only a few weeks (three!), it feels like an eternity since we last saw each other. I also can't shake the thought that maybe Seattle caused him to realize how big a loser I am. Maybe he's a different Seth—or maybe I'm a different Charlie? Or worse, we're both different and won't even recognize each other anymore.

"Oh, here he comes! Hurry, hide!" Susan says.

I dash to the baggage claim carousel—the only one in Butte—and turn my back to him. I sneak peeks over my shoulder. The door to the gate opens, and Seth appears, as handsome as ever. Not sure what I was expecting, but I'm glad he hasn't changed. Susan waves him down.

Susan squeezes him once he gets to the baggage area. He hasn't seen me yet, which is just what Susan and I want. It's my moment, and in the huddling crowd, I walk past and bump him in the shoulder. "Watch it," I say in a deep voice.

"You watch it." He turns to face me, and his eyes light up.

"Oh yeah? What are you going to do about it?" I keep the ruse going.

"Charlie!" He laughs and gives me a hug. My feet briefly lift off the ground. "It's so great to see you." He laughs again. "You had me going for a minute. What are you doing here?"

I nod to Susan. "Your mom thought I should come surprise you." I suddenly regret saying that. I want credit for coming. I don't want him to think I couldn't have thought about something like this on my own.

He doesn't seem to pick up on anything negative. "I'm so glad you did."

"See, Charlie? I told you he'd be happy to see you. Perhaps a bit happier than seeing his own mother."

Seth smiles.

I smile.

Susan smiles.

We all probably look like a bunch of smiling goons. But I like it. This feels more like a family than anything else I've felt in a long time.

Seth looks me in the eyes. He winks.

# SMALL BLACK BIRD

•••••

The ride back on the winding mountain road to Whitehall in the dark of night, through the forests of Montana, with Seth sitting next to me in the backseat, is magical.

Between looking out the window into the stillness that is an impenetrable forest, and the constant chatter of Seth telling me about Seattle, showing me his pictures on his camera, and Susan chiming in, my universe is complete.

There are moments in life when I don't wish to be taken by aliens.

Susan pulls up in front of my dormant house, and I am shaken back to my real world. I want to hang out with Seth all night long. I want to keep driving. Keep staring out. Keep talking. Keep seeing the world. I want Seth by my side. I want Susan there too.

"I hope we'll see you tomorrow!" says Susan.

"Night, Charlie. I'll call you in the morning."

I nod, and as I close the door to the car, any remaining magic evaporates, feeling almost like it never happened at all.

The walk along the walkway and into my house is cold and sobering. But as the front door sweeps open, I hear something I haven't heard in a long time from someone inside this house: laughter. I walk to the living room, and my dad sits on his recliner—blue TV light still illuminating the room—holding a stuffed animal as Tickles tries to steal it from his grip. Tickles yelps and growls, and my dad laughs. "That all you got? Huh? Come on, dog." He finally lets the stuffed animal go, and Tickles runs into the kitchen with it.

My dad turns to me, still chuckling. "This dog. Dammit, he's a funny one."

Who is this man sitting before my eyes?

He nods and then seems to realize that he has fatherly duties. "Now, where have you been?"

"Oh. I went with Susan to pick up Seth from the Butte airport."

"Who and who?"

"Just my best friend and his mom. She works at the nursing home with Grandma."

"You have a best friend? Why have I never heard about them before?"

I shrug. Though, I know the reason, and I don't think any rocket scientist is needed to understand why, so I'm guessing he knows why too.

"Why don't you let me into your life, Charlie?"

I stand there. Keeping quiet would be the best solution here. But sometimes people don't want you to keep quiet.

"Answer me."

"Because . . . you're never around."

"What are you talking about? I'm around every day."

He stands up, and I follow him to the kitchen.

Tickles is under the old metal-legged table that we have in the center of the room. He's wrestling around with the toy and making growling noises.

My dad fills up a glass of water at the faucet. He turns toward the table and takes a drink. "You know? I wonder if Tickles is ticklish."

Huh. How have I never had that thought before?

My dad bends down and reaches for the stuffed animal again. Tickles growls, but my dad manages to get both the stuffed animal and the real animal out from under the table. He picks Tickles up, and the dog quickly forgets about the stuffed animal as he's flipped onto his back. My dad holds Tickles like a baby and tickles his bare stomach. The dog squirms to get righted.

"I don't think he's ticklish," I say.

"That's only the first spot to try. What about under the ears?"

I'm suddenly jealous of the dog.

The sky again seems so black, but there I stand, looking out to the Great Beyond. I'm not sure I'm searching for a UFO at the moment. I can't really say what I'm looking for. Maybe I'm only trying to see? But see what?

Maybe standing at this window is now more of a nightly ritual?

I'm wondering what Seth is up to. Is he sleeping? Unpacking? Should I text or call him?

He said he'd talk to me tomorrow, so I need to be okay with that.

I'm still looking out the window when I see a small black bird fly spastically around my backyard. I can't tell you why I can see a black bird when it's night. I know it doesn't make sense, but I see it. And he is flying around like he's drunk or dizzy.

I see the bird fly into one of the larger tree branches and fall to the ground. Is the bird sick? I wonder if I should go outside and see, but I'm wondering if I can even do anything for the bird.

It's weird, because anytime before tonight I would've run out there without regard to consequences. In fact, I have. Many times. I've tried nursing many animals back to health. A bird, once. A sick squirrel. A dying rabbit. Even a frog. But as I stand looking out the window, I realize that I don't have much control over anything. And I have even less control over myself. My life without Seth felt lonely, but now that he's back in town, I feel confused. Things feel suddenly more complicated.

I try to see if the small black bird is moving in the grass, but I don't see anything except darkness. I look at my phone and hope that Seth has texted me, but he hasn't.

I mope over to bed, and I'm lying there quietly in my soft sheets when guilt hits me. I know I can't go to sleep without checking on the bird. Even if I know I can't do anything to save him.

My dad seems to have gone to bed, because the lights are out and the TV is off.

At the spot where the bird fell, I scan the ground and see nothing. Nothing at all. Not even the remains of a bird. I scratch my head because I could've sworn I saw a bird fall. A small black bird fell from the sky, and no one was there to catch him, and now he's gone. I look up at the stars twinkling above me, feeling like they're closer than they really are, and then head back to my room. I check my phone one last time. Hoping.

# DESIRE NEVER DIES

·····

The sun is setting, and I'm walking down main street with Seth. This is the first time we've hung out since he got back. "You want to go swimming?" he asks.

"Swimming?"

His phone vibrates. "Oh, hey, look at that," he says with a smile. "Jennifer is having a party. She wants me to go."

My heart flutters. Jennifer Bennett?

"Jennifer Bennett?"

"Yeah," he says distractedly as he texts a response back.

So many questions are going through my mind right now. Why is Seth talking to Jennifer Bennett? How well does he know her? Are they good friends? And why am I not invited? And would he rather hang out with her or me, if it came down to a decision? And why do I care?

"Want to go?" Seth asks.

"What? Me? I'm invited?"

Seth shrugs. "Sure. Why not?"

"How many times do I have to tell you that no one in this town likes me?"

Seth smiles. "I like you. So there's at least one person."

I laugh. "Okay. But how many others?"

Seth shrugs again. "Let's find out."

I shake my head. "I already know the answer."

"I'll be there with you. Nothing will happen." Seth nudges me in the arm. "Come on. She said it was a small group." He looks me in the eyes. "Please? It could be fun. Plus, Jennifer Bennett is hosting. She'll, like, have to talk to you. Maybe you can even say a few words back."

I smile. It's true. She'll have to talk to me, and maybe I'll finally be able to talk to her, and step one of my mission could possibly be complete.

Jennifer Bennett's backyard is beautiful, with large green trees and white lights hung throughout. It's almost like a mini oasis in a barren world. There's even a decent-size fishpond off to the side.

I sit down on one of the patio chairs by the fire pit. There are only four other people here, making this a pretty small party. And no one seemed to really mind when they saw me. As Seth and I made our way into her backyard, she hugged him tightly (yes, I had to look away) and said, "It's so good to see you! How was your trip?" She saw me and let go of Seth. "Hi, Charlie."

I nodded. When it became apparent that I wasn't going to talk, Seth cut in and said, "He's my plus one." Then he winked at me.

I wasn't entirely sure about his joke, but I didn't dwell too much on it.

Jennifer took hold of Seth's arm and said, "There's so much we have to talk about. Let's go inside and get drinks."

That was then. He's been with her ever since. They're inside her house, and I feel weird about going into someone's house uninvited. Even if there is a small party happening. So instead I am by the fire pit with Alex. He keeps glancing at me like he wants to say something.

The moment is getting more and more awkward, so I say, "How do you know Jennifer?"

"Newspaper."

"Ah." I study him but then look at the fire. If he doesn't want to talk, I can busy myself. I've spent a lifetime doing that. I study the flames.

"Why're you here?" he asks, breaking my trance.

"Newspaper," I say, though we both know I'm not in the newspaper class. I turn and walk through the grass to her back porch, trying to lose the constant feeling that I'm out of my element. I shouldn't be here. I'm a fraud. Heading to Jennifer's house, I am dying to know what Seth is doing with Jennifer, and that's when it hits me. Seth is doing something with Jennifer!

I nervously open the back door to Jennifer's house and peek my head in to see what's going on, but the kitchen is empty. The dining room is empty. "Hello?"

My word comes back to me. So I open the door wider.

I hear laughter coming from down the hallway, so I trudge off in that direction. I realize that Seth and Jennifer are in her room, and I lean against the wall to listen. I don't want to interrupt them, but I also want to interrupt them. Though, I secretly want to hear what they're talking about before I interrupt. I want them to confirm that I shouldn't be here. That Seth doesn't really want me around. Even though I know it's a ridiculous thought.

All I can hear is laughing, and then I hear Seth say, "I better go find Charlie."

"Can I ask, What do you see in him?" asks Jennifer.

My heart beats out of my chest.

A toilet nearby flushes, and the door opens. Samantha sees me listening and leaning up against the wall. "What are you doing, loser?" she asks.

"Me?"

She's standing in front of me. Arms crossed. Blinking. "Uh, yeah."

"Uh. Waiting for the bathroom."

"Ugh. Whatever." She walks into Jennifer's bedroom. "Creepo Charlie out there was spying on you."

Both Seth and Jennifer come out into the hallway. I shake my head. "I was just waiting for the bathroom."

Seth's face grows red. "Did you hear anything?"

I wonder if I should say yes or no. I mean, I didn't really hear anything. But maybe I should claim to have heard it all so that he confesses to something? Frankly, I don't fully understand what's happening.

Despite wanting to say yes, I shake my head.

Seth breathes a huge sigh of relief.

I point to the bathroom. "I'm just gonna . . ." I head to the bathroom.

I'm standing around the fire again, but this time Seth is by my side. Jennifer is across from me.

"Let's get the party started!" I hear. Shouts and calls of

"Whoop!" follow, and I turn to see the Ass Trio walking into Jennifer's backyard.

"Shit," I whisper under my breath. But they haven't seen me yet. I'm especially concerned about Psych, who will probably want to kick my ass. I turn to Seth. I find myself tugging the sleeve of his T-shirt. "We need to go."

Jennifer is already heading over to them. They are holding at least four six-packs of beer. Where did they get them, I wonder. But actually I don't care, because I just want to get away before they see me.

"Don't worry, Charlie. They won't bother you."

I also remember the last thing Joey told me: "Next time bring your boyfriend."

I'm worried for Seth as much as I'm worried for myself.

I pull him to me and whisper. "They want to beat us both up."

"Is that right?" Seth looks at Joey. He doesn't seem frightened by that news.

"Come on, Seth. Let's go. It's for our own protection."

Seth isn't interested in leaving, and I plead with him before the three assholes get to the fire. The night is dark enough that they can probably only see our silhouettes, and I guarantee that they aren't expecting to see Charlie Dickens at a party thrown by Jennifer Bennett. I'm still not sure I believe it. And I'm still unnoticed.

"I have to go," I say. And I dart away from the fire pit, in the opposite direction of the Ass Trio.

I hear Seth shout out, "Charlie?"

And I hear Joey say, "Is that little Charles Dickens?"

But I'm gone before I can hear anything else. This is not the summer adventure I was hoping for. I don't want to leave Seth, but if he wants to put himself in danger, there's nothing I can do to stop him.

I quickly walk past the quiet shuttered storefronts. I want to get home before anything can possibly happen.

I hear Seth running up behind me. "Charlie! Wait!" He's slightly out of breath.

I can't stop thinking about what's stuck in my head. "What's going on?" I ask as I keep walking.

Seth reaches me and grabs my shoulder. "What do you mean?"

"Why did you not want me to know what you were talking about with Jennifer?"

Seth studies my sincere face. "Because."

"Oh." I feel like he's completely disregarding my feelings or something. "I see."

Seth turns away. "I'd rather not say right now. Is that okay?"

I nod. But now I just want to know more than ever.

A question picks at my chest. "Do you love her?"

"What?" Seth seems shocked. "She's just a friend, Charlie."

Do I believe him? I nod again. "Well, I better get home."

"Can I join you?"

"Don't you want to stay at the party? You seemed pretty intent on staying near imminent danger."

"I don't want to be there if you're not there to keep me company. And I'm not afraid of Joey."

I find myself pissed. "Seems like Jennifer Bennett is enough company for you." I walk away in a huff.

Seth catches up with me. "Charlie, come on. That's not fair. I haven't seen or talked to her in weeks."

I shake my head. "Whatever."

"Why are you mad?" he asks.

I don't know. I have no idea why I'm so pissed off right now. But I am. "I just want to be left alone," I say. Seth stops walking with me. I notice that and stop walking and turn to him. *What am I doing? I'm messing up my friendship for no good reason.* "I'm sorry. Can I talk to you tomorrow?"

"I'd like that."

I study the concern on his face, and yet I just have to be alone even if I don't really know why. So I walk away. Tonight's sky on the lonely road back home: *Torn to Pieces by Some Cosmic Undoing.*

# NO ONE'S INNOCENT WHEN HEARTS ARE BROKEN

·····

My bed doesn't feel as comfy tonight, but I enjoy petting Tickles, who is lying on my bed at the moment. I'm surprised my dad hasn't stolen Tickles for his bed again. Though, he's not home yet, so I imagine it could still happen.

You know, it feels pathetic to always be home earlier than your parent. At least that's how I feel. I should be the one out late.

My phone buzzes, and it's Seth.

I don't answer. I don't know why I'm so pissed off, but I am. It's bothering me that I'm so angry with my best friend.

"You'll be my best friend, won't you, Tickles?" I scratch behind his ears, and he seems happy. "We need to go see Geoffrey tomorrow. I bet you miss him, huh? He's been in the hospital for far too long."

My phone buzzes again.

I hit ignore. Besides, it's about time to look out the window and up to the sky.

# CHOKE

.....

It's early afternoon, and I haven't made contact with Seth yet. Instead I'm walking with Tickles through the nursing home. Well, trying to walk through the nursing home. A bigger lady with a blanket over her lap in a wheelchair says, "What a beautiful dog. Can I pet him?" After five minutes of talking with her and letting her pet Tickles, I say we have to get going.

Not ten feet later an old man is hobbling down the hallway with a cane. "What in the holy hell is that thing?" he asks, and pokes at Tickles with his cane. "Rose? Come out here. This kid's walking a robot. Now I've seen it all."

Tickles attacks the cane and then rears back and growls. "Hey, leave the dog alone. Come on, Tickles."

I don't see Susan at the nurse's station or on the way to my grandma's room. Maybe she has the weekend off.

"Knock, knock," I say as I enter Grandma's cave. Today we're going to start the puzzle that I brought her last time.

She turns and smiles. "Charlie, my dear."

"What? Did you say my name, Grandma?"

She then looks absently at the wall. I shake my head, thinking it was my brain playing tricks on me.

"Look who I brought," I say, gesturing to Tickles.

Her smile grows. She puts her hand out. "Come here. Come here."

I'm starting to wonder if she's having a lucid moment. "How about some light in here?" I open the blinds and briefly check the sky. The ferocious heat wave has finally ended.

I look at the clock, and it's exactly on time. "Oh, Grandma, look at that." I point to the clock. "It's on the right time! I don't know the last time that's happened."

I grab the puzzle from the windowsill and go back to the spare chair. "How about we start our puzzle? Want to go down to the rec room?"

She turns her head away from me in defiance. I figure it's easier to just start the puzzle here than fight her on moving.

Tickles sits down by my feet.

I spread out the pieces on her rolling table. It's not ideal because it's pretty narrow, and we'll have to move the puzzle before I leave. But it's the only surface available.

"See what the picture looks like?" I hold up the box and point.

"A bridge," she says without any hint of mental confusion. And her eyes. They're clear and connecting with mine.

I smile. "That's right. So we need to find the corner and edge pieces first." I set the box down beside my chair.

"I know how to put together a puzzle, Charlie."

I look back up at her, and she's looking at her thumbs. I stare at her for a brief second. Am I going crazy? The doctor said he didn't think she'd have any more lucid moments, but I guess I'd like to think she still can.

I'm searching for pieces when she asks, "How's your father? I'm not sure I've seen him since shortly after your mother left."

I look up, startled. I'd almost believe she was saying these things if she would keep her inquisitiveness when I look at her. Instead I find her gazing into another world. A world for one.

She turns to me and stares into my eyes. "I am no longer living."

A shiver runs up my spine. "Grandma?"

"Charlie?"

Holy shit! "You're having a lucid moment? Grandma. Oh my god!"

She shakes her head. "I'm wasting away in here. In this chair. This"—she looks around the room—"is the carcass of my once grand life."

Holy shit! My grandma is having a conversation with me. That hasn't happened in more than a year. My eyes fill with tears. "That's not . . . You have a lot more to live for. It's all in your perspective."

"Why doesn't your father come visit?"

"He's . . . busy."

"Still drinking? Fishing? Ignoring the world?"

I nod. "Yeah. He hasn't been the same since, well, you know."

"Charlie." She reaches out to me. I take hold of her hand. Some of the tears are streaming down my face.

"I miss you, Grandma."

"I love you. You know that, right?"

I nod. I nod.

"You take care of yourself, Charlie. You're so special." She squeezes my hand. She smiles and then pulls her hand away. She looks out the window, and it's almost like I can see the haze fill her mind again. Her eyes become the same vacant expressionless eyes that I've grown used to.

"Do you want to continue with the puzzle?" I ask.

She tilts her head and smiles at me as if I'm some side-show curiosity.

"The puzzle, Grandma." I hand her a corner piece. And she looks at it curiously. "Put it right there." I point at a spot on the table.

As I keep searching for other edge pieces, she coughs. She doesn't stop coughing, and I look up at her. The puzzle piece is gone from her hand. "Where's the piece, Grandma? Where is it?"

I shove the chair back and stand quickly. Tickles stands and barks. Grandma's hands are grasping at her neck.

"Help! Somebody help!" I yell.

No one's coming, and I'm growing more worried. "Dammit! Somebody, please! Help!"

Finally a nurse runs into the room and asks what's happening. "Choking," is all I can say. He stands behind her. I need to learn the Heimlich maneuver, I tell myself as I watch him dislodge the puzzle piece, which flies out and lands in the pile of pieces on the table.

I swipe all the puzzle pieces back into the box. Dumb idea. The nurse helps Grandma into bed.

Fresh tears cloud my vision.

\* \* \*

I sat at the kitchen table reading a book. The house had just started to die. To become a tomb. But I didn't know it at the time. I hadn't yet fully realized what had happened or the consequences of it. Grandma was in one of her amazing outfits. She always looked so good, proper, and put together when she left her house. "Never leave your house unless you look like someone worth seeing," she said to me many times when I was growing up.

My dad was in the garage, or the backyard, or somewhere outside and not in the house.

My grandma stood in the kitchen with me. She was making some kind of casserole for dinner. "Want to help, Charlie?"

I shook my head and closed my book.

"Charlie. This has nothing to do with you."

I nodded.

"Don't for a second think it does."

I didn't. I didn't think about it for a second.

A little later I was in my parents' room looking through a trunk that my mother had kept at the foot of the bed. In it was a collection of pictures, postcards—past lives of my parents. I pulled out a picture of my parents' wedding day: my mom in her white wedding dress and hair done up, my dad in a black-and-white tuxedo, hair combed and parted on the side. They held each other around the waist at the front of the church. They smiled outward. To the others. To the photographer.

A moment, real or fake, caught forever.

I held the picture. I studied it. I wondered if there

were any signs of cracks or fissures, of what would come between this man and woman.

I couldn't find anything.

I heard my grandma and dad arguing in the kitchen.

"She needed help! And what did you do, Steve?"

"I did help."

"You were too busy in your own world to reach out. Drinking. Working all the hours you could get."

"I'm trying to care for this family."

"You couldn't care for the woman you loved."

"That's bullshit, and you know it."

"Where were you when she was going downhill? You weren't there for her. You'd yell and tell her she was an embarrassment."

"I was trying to help."

"You pushed her away."

"Get out. Get out of my house!"

I jumped when I heard a glass break. A door slam. A silence then washed over the house.

I quietly put the picture back into the trunk. Closed the lid. And went away.

# HE'S GONE

.....

I forgot the dog carrier, which seemed to work in keeping nurses off my back last time. So I pick up Tickles and tuck him under my arm and quickly trot down the hall to Geoffrey's room. When I enter, I see that it's empty. I don't see any of Geoffrey's belongings. My chest constricts.

I turn around and head back into the hall.

I look into other rooms to see if he's just been moved. I get to the nurse's station. A nurse looks busy and I don't want to interrupt, but I clear my throat. "Excuse me? Where is Geoffrey Smazinski?" My heart is beating a million miles a minute.

When the nurse turns around she frowns. "Haven't I told you no dogs before, young man? I will ban you from this hospital if I see that dog here one more time."

My face flushes red. "Yes, sorry."

She turns, picks up a blue folder, opens it, and says to the wall, "He's being taken home."

"What?" I ask excitedly. I look down at Tickles and

bounce him. "Did you hear that? He's going home! Isn't that great?"

Tickles barks and squirms.

"No dogs," says the nurse as she glares at me.

I run out of the hospital. I can't get to Geoffrey's quickly enough.

On the way to Geoffrey's my phone vibrates.

Seth.

I can't continue to ignore my best friend. So I answer. "You won't believe the day I've had."

Seth sounds like he's been crying. "Charlie? Do you hate me?"

I stop walking in the middle of the sidewalk. "What? No. Why would I hate you?"

He sniffs. "That's what I was wondering. But last night . . . and you've been ignoring me."

I dig my foot into the cement. "Yeah. Sorry. I guess I was just upset last night. I don't know what got into me."

"So we're good, then?"

I hesitate briefly. "Yes. We're good."

I know it doesn't sound possible, but I hear him smile. That makes me smile. "Want to hang out tonight?" he asks.

I nod. Then I realize he can't see me, and say, "Yes. I'd love to."

"Just us. You and me. And no other jerks."

I laugh. "No other jerks."

It feels like a weight is lifted from my shoulders, and relief washes over me when I see Geoffrey on the green couch again. It's like the world has corrected itself.

Tickles, I think, is relieved too. But he runs his little butt to the kitchen to eat some food and drink some water.

"Charlie!" Geoffrey says upon seeing me enter his house. "How are ya?"

"I should be asking you that." He actually looks a little thinner. Whether that was a side effect of the infection, I don't know.

"Oh, I'm great. Haven't felt better."

I'm pretty sure that's a lie. I'm sure there was a time when he felt better, when he wasn't so heavy, but I don't say anything.

"Thanks for taking care of Tickles."

"I'm actually a little sad to lose him. He makes for good company." I hear Tickles chomping on the food in the kitchen.

"Well, I'm sure he's sad to be back to this stinky old place." Geoffrey smiles. Then he looks down and then back up at me. "Yes, sir," he says, with a strong commitment in his voice. "I'm going to turn my life around. More exercise. Healthier food. The hospital visit was a wake-up call for me."

"That's great news." I'm excited for Geoffrey. Maybe someday he can go on walks with me and Tickles.

# SPLITTING IN A FLASH

.....

Seth dribbles a basketball around in his driveway. He shoots from the grass at the far end, and the ball hits the rim and bounces out.

"Just warming up?" I say as I ride up to him.

Seth laughs. "Came with the house. Want to go swimming?"

"You're really pushing this swimming thing."

"What good is summer without swimming?"

"The nearest pool is in Butte."

"I was thinking like a river or lake?"

"Nothing super close. There's Delmoe Lake up in the mountains. Not sure how we'll get there."

"My mom's car?"

"And I don't have swimming trunks or a towel with me."

"Anything else?"

I smile and shake my head. Seth tosses me the ball. "I'll be right back." He runs inside, and I'm left holding the basketball, which feels awkward. I look at the basket and steady my aim. I throw the ball, and it hits the backboard like a brick. I pretend that I didn't just do that, and let the ball roll into the grass.

Seth comes out with his backpack. "Bad news. My mom won't let me take the car."

"So we can't go?"

"Not there. Is there like a creek around?"

"A creek? I mean, there's a small one a few miles out of town. But if we don't have a car?"

"Then it's a good thing we both have bikes."

"And swimming trunks?"

Seth pats his backpack. He's ready.

"Fine," I say.

As we're riding our bikes out of town on the side of a two-lane highway, I say, "This is kind of dangerous."

"Great, right?"

I mumble to myself, "Sure. Great. As long as we don't get smashed by a car."

"What was that?" he asks.

"Nothing."

After the fourth mile Seth is a few yards behind me, trying to keep up, and is groaning with every pedal. "Almost there," I say.

We reach the creek, and he quickly scans the area. "It's like one foot deep."

"It's a creek."

"How are we going to swim in that?"

"I don't know."

"I've got an idea."

I follow Seth as he walks a few yards down the bank of the creek. He turns to me and asks, "What are you doing?"

"Ah. Following you?"

"I'm trying to change over here."

"Oh. Sorry."

"Here." He throws me a pair of swimming trunks. "My old ones. I think they'll fit you."

When we both have our swimming trunks on and our shoes and socks off, Seth wades into the creek. "Oh! Shit. This is a lot colder than I thought it'd be."

"You're not from around here, are you?"

Seth smirks at me. "Are you going to help?"

"What are you doing?"

"I'm going to build a dam."

"A what?"

"A dam."

I was just making sure that that was what he said. "Not sure that's a good idea."

"Charlie, just come help."

I watch Seth dig around in the water, which is about up to his knees. He finds rocks, picks them up, and places them a few feet downstream, where it's just a tad more shallow.

"Fine." I wade into the shockingly cold water and help build the wall of rocks, which after about fifteen minutes is really starting to stop some water.

Seth says, "If we can't find a deep spot to swim in, we'll make one."

The spot we make doesn't ever get exactly deep, but the water ends up three or so inches higher. Or maybe we just clear away three inches of rocks from the bottom. Either way, we can sit in the water, which is what we are doing. I'm shivering as I listen to Seth, and I move my arms periodically to keep warm. His feet occasionally graze my feet. Sometimes his hands graze my legs. But I figure it's just the small confines of our "pool."

The sun is starting to set.

"I want to take more pictures of you," he says.

"Of me? Why?"

"Like, pictures of you just doing random stuff."

"Um. I guess," I say with a clenched jaw. My body shivers.

"Ready to get out?"

I nod vigorously.

We wade out of the water, and Seth grabs the two towels and tosses one to me. He drops down to the grass near the creek. "Ahhh."

I stand there trying to dry off as my entire body continues to shiver.

"Join me." He pats the grass.

I hesitate before I sit. Then I watch Seth lie on his back and look up at the sky as it changes colors. It's amazing, the various colors that show off when the sky moves from blue to black.

After some moments of silence, Seth says, "I don't get it."

"What?"

"What is so intriguing to you about UFOs? Like, why are you always searching for them?"

"I'm not."

"Charlie, I know you better than that."

I sigh. "Fine. You won't make fun of me?"

"Promise."

Though it's hard for me to say any of this out loud, I don't want to keep any more secrets from Seth. I take a deep breath. "I want to be the first person to fully document the existence of aliens. Because they do exist."

Seth turns to me and gives me a *Come on* look.

"See all those stars?" I say.

"Yeah."

"That's, like, not even one one-billionth of the stars in the universe. And we happen to be the only planet that has life? Hardly."

Seth scrunches up his face.

"Something wrong?" I ask.

"I mean, it's amazing that you want to be the first to prove that aliens exist. But that doesn't really tell me why."

I sit silently next to him. I feel guilty about keeping my reasons a secret. Even when I want to tell my secrets, it's hard to actually do it. Life is weird. How could the same information cause me pain if I tell it and then pain if I don't tell it?

Seth sits up, his hand brushing mine, and suddenly I find our shoulders touching.

I become aware of the creek bubbling as I turn to Seth, who seems to be staring at me longingly.

"What is it?" I ask nervously.

He shakes his head as he holds my gaze a second longer.

The night sky is cloudy on the ride back to town. There are so many mysteries in life. I'm starting to believe there are more mysteries in my own life here on Earth than there are in the vast universe. There are so many unanswered questions. So many alien moments with even the people I know.

# A FACE AT THE EDGE
# OF THE BREAK

.....

When I get home, I am truly exhausted. Between Grandma choking, and all the excitement with Geoffrey, and then the biking and swimming with Seth, I can barely keep from crashing onto the couch and sleeping there for the night.

My dad is in front of the TV and tells me to come talk to him. I stand next to him. "What are you doing? Sit on the couch." He's mostly staring at the TV.

I shuffle to the couch. He first tells me that he's going fishing tomorrow but that he'll be back tomorrow night. After some gunshots on TV, he says, "Heard about your grandma. They called."

My chest tightens. Is he talking about today or when I broke her out?

"Maybe don't bring puzzles to her anymore."

My chest relaxes.

"And where's Tickles?" he asks.

"Oh. Geoffrey got to come home today."

"Glad for Geoffrey, but I was enjoying that dog." My dad turns off the TV and stands up. The house is completely dark. "I'm off to bed. Come give me a hug."

I hug him and head to my room. As I sit at my desk, eyes barely open, I see an email from Meridian X on my laptop.

> Hi, Charlie,
> I'll be traveling through Whitehall
> tomorrow. Wanted to know if you'd like to
> grab coffee? We could swap stories.
> Let me know. It'll be around 2 p.m.
> Thanks,
> Meridian X
> **Owner/Operator, MontanaUFOSightings.
> com**
> ****Buy My Book! Montana UFO
> Sightings****

I lean back in my chair and wonder why she wants to have coffee with me. But I'm all for it.

I stand up and slog over to my window. I search the darkness for some kind of light. For some kind of sound. For some kind of something. I stand there for as long as I can. But I just can't stay awake any longer, so I slouch to my bed.

My dad is gone by the time I wake up.

# BETTER WITHOUT

· · · · ·

The only coffee shop open in Whitehall on a Sunday is called Sweet Honey Café, at the far end of main street. It looks like a cottage, and inside is an overwhelming amount of floral designs—from the table covers to the wallpaper to the fake flowers in the middle of the tables. A woman named Mary Jo owns and runs the place. She used to be a good friend of my grandma's. Maybe she's still a friend of my grandma's, but I'm not sure how that works when the other person is unaware of the friendship.

I walk into the empty café, and Mary Jo comes out from the back. "Charlie, oh my! It's been quite a while. Good to see you. How's Eloise doing? I need to get over and see her. I've been saying that for a while, but I need to just do it. Though, after working all day, it's hard to close the café and not go home and crash."

I stand there, smiling, with my hands in my pockets. "She's doing well," I say.

"Oh, that's wonderful." She flips the kitchen towel she's

holding over her shoulder. "What can I get you?"

"I'm going to meet someone, so I'm just going to wait for now." I suddenly regret having a meeting with another alien/UFO person in a place where I know the owner. *Charlie Dickens, do you ever think?* I don't want people to start suspecting that I'm slipping . . . like my mom.

I sit by the window and look out. My phone buzzes with a text from Seth. You'll never guess what I saw!!! OMG!

What!?! I reply.

A light. A big bright blinding light last night around 2am.

My heart jumps. Seriously!? I need more info!

I'll tell you later. In person?

Okay. I'm meeting with the website lady shortly.

The UFO website lady?

That one.

Really? That's cool. What's the meeting for?

I hear gravel crunch, and I look up to see a green Subaru park in front of the café. The woman driving is in her midforties, with hair that is shooting out in all directions, kind of like Albert Einstein.

She looks around the café once she enters, and there's only me. I wave. She pulls down her sunglasses and glances at me. Then she puts them back on, smiles, and walks over.

"Charlie? I wasn't expecting a teenager."

I shrug. My hands are folded like I'm being interviewed or something. "Yeah, it's just me."

She sits. "No, no, I think it's great. Someone so young involved in such a complicated subject."

"You could say it kind of found me."

"I'd love to hear your story." She looks around as Mary Jo comes over.

"What can I get you two?"

We order some coffees, and Mary Jo heads back to the counter.

Meridian X, still wearing sunglasses, looks at me. I think.

"So is your name really Meridian X?" My leg keeps bouncing, though I'm trying not to focus on it.

"What do you think, Charlie?"

I press my hand to my thigh. "No?"

"I have my legal name and the name I prefer to go by, which is Meridian X." She studies me a minute. "You don't like your name, do you?"

"Yeah, I like it." How would she know whether I like my name or not?

"Don't lie to me. If you could pick your name, what would it be?"

"How do you know I don't like my name?" I think this is an odd conversation to be having with an (almost) complete stranger.

"Well, when you wrote me back after I asked you whether you wanted your first or first and last name on the website, you said something to the effect of, 'Please. Do *not* post my last name.'"

"Maybe I just don't want people to know I'm into watching aliens."

"Possible, yes. But most people who spot something want credit for it. So you're saying you wouldn't change your name?"

"I don't know. Probably not." It's a weird thing to ask, because I think of a name as something concrete, something that follows you throughout life and is a reminder of a person after death.

"You are always free to change your name," she says. Thankfully, she takes her sunglasses off and places them on the table. I didn't like when I couldn't see her eyes.

I nod. I'm not sure why I've never thought about it before. I mean, why do I have to keep anything that anyone has given me? My name is wrought with baggage. And history. On the one hand, that's good. On the other, it haunts me. Maybe I will change my name.

Mary Jo brings over our drinks and places them delicately on her floral tabletop.

Meridian X smiles. She takes a sip of her coffee.

I'm not sure how much cream or sugar to put into my coffee, as I can count on one finger the number of times I've had coffee. So I dump half the cream into it, and then open five packs of sugar.

I take a sip. It's actually pretty good.

Meridian X laughs. "You ever had coffee before?"

I feel awkward and take another gulp of my coffee. "My friend Seth said he saw a light last night."

Meridian X jerks forward, and her eyes light up. "Was it like the light you saw?"

"No idea. He just texted me about it."

"Well, get him down here!"

"Really?" I eye her.

"Yes!"

I pull out my phone.

\* \* \*

My leg is still bouncing, but for another reason. I'm on my third cup of coffee, and I feel good.

Meridian X is sipping from her second cup and we're discussing my encounter, which she already heard about through our emails, when she says, "Did you know that this coming week has historically been the most active week?"

I shake my head. "What do you mean?"

"In studying paranormal activity from history, this last week in July measures as the most active. The most UFO sightings, the most alien abductions, the most, well, everything."

My heart pounds. "Really? Why? What is it about this week?"

Meridian X looks at me, dead serious. "The aliens like warmer weather."

I'm contemplating whether there's any validity to this, when she busts out laughing.

"I'm kidding, Charlie. I have no idea. I just know that this week is the most active. So be on the lookout. Okay?"

I will definitely be on the lookout. The door opens, and in walks Seth with his camera around his neck, and I get an idea. This will be the week of our summer adventure.

# HEADING FOR WATERLOO

·····

"Okay, so I was just dinking around on the internet, right?" says Seth. Both Meridian X and I are rapt with attention. Her chin is resting on her fisted hand. "And all of a sudden, out of the blue, there's this loud noise. It sounds like thunder. I take off my headphones, because I could hear it through them, and I sit there for a second, wondering what is happening. Then I see this bright flash, almost like someone took a picture of me. But it was larger than that. Like they took a picture of the whole town. So . . . I get up and look outside, but it was like nothing had happened at all. The town was still."

I'm sitting next to Seth, arms crossed, wondering why I didn't hear or see anything myself, but I was sawing logs. Though, if it was as loud as Seth explained, then why didn't I wake up? Could I have slept through the aliens coming to get me?

Could this explain why I'm still here? I keep sleeping through their arrivals?

Meridian X's eyes look like a child's on Christmas morning, and I find myself wondering why she is so fascinated with UFOs and alien encounters. Especially as a middle-aged adult, where it's probably more looked down upon than if you're a fourteen-year-old high school student.

"Why didn't you call me immediately?" I ask Seth.

"Because you were sleeping. And you put your phone on silent when you go to bed."

This is true. Shit.

"Well, this is just absolutely fascinating," says Meridian X. "Could it be the same UFO?" She stares at both of us. "Maybe it's here for one of you?" Her eyes are genuine, and I can't help but feel my nerves tingling all over my body. My leg bounces a thousand miles a minute.

Meridian X says, "Your story reminded me of the same kind of light I encountered when I was abducted."

"Abducted?" asks Seth. "Is that . . . Wait. Did they probe you?"

Meridian X laughs. "Want to hear the story?"

We both nod vigorously.

"I was abducted in a church. In a church basement, to be precise. It happened when I was a little girl, no older than ten. It was Sunday morning, and I was in Sunday school with our teacher. What was his name? Well, anyway, the teacher—Todd something. Or was it something Todd? It doesn't matter. He dismissed the class but asked me to stay back and help him straighten up the room. I gladly helped, and I was putting the colored pencils back in the boxes when a bright flash lit up the room."

"I thought you were in a basement?" asks Seth.

"Shhh!" I say.

"I was. But each room had three tiny rectangular windows at the top of the wall to let in some natural light. But that's why it was so concerning—that so much light came through such small windows.

"Right after the light, which I'll admit kind of stunned me a bit, there was an enormous crack. Kind of like those fireworks that explode into a palm tree and crackle on the way down.

"I remember my Sunday school teacher moaning. Something was giving him pain. But when I turned to see if he was injured, I saw an alien. Standing right in front of me. At first I thought that I'd jumped and screamed, but actually I couldn't move at all. And no sound could come out of my mouth."

My butt feels glued to the seat.

"This is creepy," says Seth.

"Quit interrupting!" I say.

"Someone's touchy," he replies.

I glare at Seth and then turn back to Meridian X so that she can continue.

"The alien put out his hand—and I was suddenly no longer frozen. I took it, and we walked what felt like up and through the wall. But I know that can't be right. That'd be impossible. But that's what I remember.

"Next thing I know, I'm being fanned awake by my Sunday school teacher on the carpet of the room. He said I had fainted."

"What? What kind of ending is that?" asks Seth. "You don't remember the actual abduction or the spaceship or anything?"

Meridian X shakes her head and takes a sip of coffee. "Wish I did. I'd be a millionaire."

I finally have to ask a question. "And no one else saw or heard anything?"

She shakes her head again. "The few people I asked just laughed at me. So I quickly gave up on asking. They thought it was a vision I had while I was passed out. But the thing is, I'd never passed out before that occurrence, and I haven't passed out since."

Seth and I stand in the parking lot, waving to Meridian X as she drives away.

There are some dark clouds right above us, but only a few, so it doesn't look like the storm will last.

"Ready to go?" Seth asks.

I notice the camera hanging around his neck again. "Wait. Do you have pictures?"

"I have lots of pictures."

"No, of last night."

"Oh, uh . . . I actually didn't have my camera handy. I was in bed, and by the time I got up and saw what was happening, the thing was gone."

"Oh," I say, looking down at the gravel parking lot, the few weeds here and there, the crumbling cement car bumpers.

"Let's go," he says with excitement.

"Where are we going?"

"Anywhere. We have my mom's car."

Now we're on the old highway heading to Waterloo, a town smaller than Whitehall (if you can believe that). It's only a handful of minutes away, and only a handful of people live there.

Seth is quiet for a moment, and then says, "Do you believe her? The story about being abducted?" Seth looks like he can't decide what to believe. "It just seems . . . I don't know. Off."

"You don't believe her?"

"I don't think so. I mean, maybe she just had a dream. We know she passed out. Doesn't that make more sense?"

"But that's not what she believes."

Seth is quiet and thoughtful, and the silence builds. I look at him. The road. Him. He turns to me and smiles. "Does that make a difference?" he asks.

"Does it matter to her if we believe her or not?"

"Hmm. I can't think this deeply on an empty stomach. How about some pizza?"

Fat drops of rain start to hit the windshield.

"Pizza sounds amazing," I say.

We reach the turnoff for the "town" of Waterloo, which is literally a dirt road. This should give a sense of the size, when the only road to get to a town isn't even paved. Seth looks at me and says, "I've never been to Waterloo."

"You don't want to go."

"Let's check it out."

I shake my head. "It's depressing. There's, like, four houses with old people. And some horses."

"It has to be bigger than that."

"Nope."

As he drives through the "town," he says, "There's nothing here. What makes it a town?"

"It has a postal code."

"Seriously?"

"Do you know what 'waterloo' means?" I ask.

Seth shakes his head. "Isn't 'loo' what they call a bath-room in England?" His face is serious.

"Really?" I ask.

Seth laughs. "So the word means 'water toilet.'"

I laugh. "Water toilet? No. 'Defeat.'"

"What?" Seth turns the car around. "Let's get out of here."

"To 'meet your waterloo' is to be defeated."

"How do you know that?"

"How do we know anything?" I ask.

"What kind of an answer is that?"

"An okay one." I smirk as Seth shakes his head at me.

We leave the town of Waterloo in the distance.

# THE PLAN AND SOME PIZZA

•••••

We're sitting at a table waiting for the large pepperoni pizza with anchovies (because Seth is weird), when I scoot to the edge of my chair. "I have an idea for our summer adventure. Meridian X told me that this week is historically the most active week for alien and UFO activity."

"There's such a thing?"

"What do you say we go on a weeklong camping trip, starting tomorrow? But not just camping, searching for aliens?"

He smirks and says, "Just us? I don't know much about camping."

"I know enough. And I can teach you."

He leans back and thinks. "Hmm."

"We can make s'mores."

"Okay. I'm in."

We both laugh, and the door opens right next to our table. There's a person silhouetted against the blinding bright sun that has emerged after the rainstorm. After the door closes, Jennifer Bennett approaches. My heart beats irregularly, and I don't want to look at her directly for fear of embarrassment and shame, but I don't want to look away, because she's the most beautiful girl in the universe. She's wearing short shorts and yellow sunglasses, which she's pulling off when she says, "Seth."

Seth jumps up and hugs Jennifer.

A pang of jealousy stabs my chest, but I'm trying to play it cool. Did he know she was coming? It feels like he's not really that surprised to see her.

"Hi, Charlie," says Jennifer, sitting down at our table.

"Oh, um, hi." I turn away awkwardly and stare at the sunlight shining on the five-room motel across the street. Would you believe this is the most I've said to her all year? I know, I know.

But watching them talk, I'm wondering why Seth wouldn't tell me that Jennifer was coming to pizza, unless he didn't want me to question him about it. And he wouldn't want me to question him about it if he's dating her. Especially because he's known all along how much I like her.

"Isn't that right, Charlie?" asks Seth.

I look over. "Huh?"

"The weeklong camping trip?"

"Uh-huh. Wait. What about it?"

Seth laughs. "We're going on one. Remember?"

I nod.

Jennifer looks excited. "Oh, that sounds like such a good time. What are you two going to do?"

Seth's eyes go wide. "Oh, uh . . ."

My heart races. "We're just . . . going camping." I can't have her knowing about the alien thing.

"That's all," Seth says.

Jennifer sits back. "Riiiight."

My face burns. She suspects something. Oh god.

The manager/owner/cook/cashier brings the large pepperoni pizza (with anchovies) out to our table. Seth sniffs. "Smells goooooood."

"It smells like cat breath," I say. But I still grab a slice.

# RADIO SILENCE

·····

When I get home, I see that my dad is still not home from fishing. Usually he's home by this hour. Especially because the guys don't usually fish in the dark.

I call my dad, and it goes straight to voice mail. I don't have any of my dad's friends' numbers. He might just be at the bar, I figure. My phone rings.

"Yes?"

"Hello to you too, Charlie," Seth says.

"Sorry. I'm frustrated."

"By what?" asks Seth.

"Nothing. What's up?"

"Some bad news . . . My mom isn't too keen on me being gone for the whole week. She said one night at first, but I got her up to two."

"Two nights?" My heart sinks. "That's hardly anything."

"I know. But it took everything I have just to get her up to two nights."

Looking around, my kitchen feels so cold and dark. "Okay," I say. "Two nights."

"Everything okay?" asks Seth. "You sound upset."

I am upset. *First, I think you're trying to take Jennifer Bennett from me. But second, maybe it's less about losing Jennifer Bennett than it is about losing you, which confuses me. Third, it feels like everywhere I turn, someone or something is against me. Two nights? How will we ever find aliens?* "I'm fine. See you tomorrow morning?"

Seth starts to say something, but I hang up. The kitchen now looks colder.

I leave my phone on the counter because I don't want to talk to Seth. I know he's going to call repeatedly, which makes me feel guilty for leaving him hanging. I don't like knowing that someone is worrying or thinking about me if I disappear. It's a responsibility I don't think I asked for. Then again, maybe being someone's friend is pretty much all about responsibility. And if that's the case, I'm the worst friend in the world, which only makes me feel guiltier.

I can't stand being in this house alone, so I head out the back door.

I see a yellow light coming from Geoffrey's house.

"Hi, Charlie," says Geoffrey, sitting on his green couch, TV blaring. "Come on in."

"How have you been?"

"Oh, great. Great."

"Been doing the exercises you're supposed to do?"

Geoffrey nods. "Every day."

A little bell is getting louder, and I smile. "Tickles, come here, boy."

Tickles runs in, and I kneel down and pet him. "Missed you," I say in my doggie/baby voice.

Geoffrey smiles. "Someday soon I'll be taking him for a walk."

"That'd be great." I pet Tickles a little more before standing up and brushing my hands off on my pants. "Oh, so I'm going camping this week. Can I take Tickles for two nights? I think he'd like getting out and about."

"Tickles would love that."

"Cool. Thanks." I sit on the recliner. "Whatcha watching?"

"Oh, just this show on World War II pilots."

"Can I watch it with you?"

"Stay as long as you'd like—I've got no one to see and nowhere to be."

As I watch the black-and-white images of the pilots flying the fighter planes, my mind drifts to Seth. He's probably calling. And I want to ask him about Jennifer Bennett. They seem so close that I can barely stand it. When did that happen? Where was I? Does he have this whole unknown side to him?

When I get home, I check my phone. Three calls from Seth and four texts. Nothing from my dad.

I go up to my room and call my dad. Voice mail again. I call Seth, but hang up before it rings. I decide to text him instead. Hey. Sorry. Was helping Geoffrey and forgot my phone. Tomorrow at 8? My house?

I feel like you're mad at me.

I am. No. I'm good.

Seriously?

Seriously. I'd tell you if I was mad.

Why am I such a coward? This is going to be a long two days. Unless we get visitors. Fingers crossed.

# PART THREE

## LOST POLARIS

# ALL GOOD SUMMER ADVENTURES START WITH AN ALARM

.....

I hit my alarm clock and open my eyes. Then I reach for my glasses. It's six thirty a.m., and the sun is shining through the window. (I stopped closing my blinds after the first time I saw the light. I figured, why close the blinds if all I want to do is see out?)

Seth is meeting me here at nine a.m. now . . . which took some work on my part, because he wanted to meet at noon after I suggested eight.

Downstairs I notice the silence and the coffee pot has the same amount of old coffee as the day before. Has he still not returned home?

At this thought, I walk to his bedroom and find his bed empty. Everything has remained in the same untouched position as the night before: the bedsheets, the half-pulled-out dresser drawer, the half-closed blinds. My heart pangs, and I call him again. But this time I leave a voice mail. "Hey, Dad. This is your son. Charlie. Um. Anyway, I don't know where you are. Or why you aren't home. I'm going camping for a couple of days with Seth. I know you haven't met him, but he's a good kid. We'll be back on Wednesday, and I'm hoping you'll be home then too." I stare at the nightstand on my mom's side of the bed, the place where her pictures were, and her jewelry box and some books. Now the nightstand is completely empty as if my dad didn't want her personal belongings around; as if he didn't want to be reminded of her.

I start to feel resentful at the awkwardness of his abandoned bedroom. I reach to press the end button, but stop. "I'm kind of pissed at you. Why did you just disappear? Why are you acting like Mom? I mean, I'm just a kid, for crying out loud. I think some fucking parental guidance isn't too much to ask for. Or maybe just someone to eat a goddamned dinner with once in a while." I hang up and slam the door to his bedroom. The old family pictures on the wall outside his room shake. We haven't taken a new family photo since my mom left. It's like, when she disappeared, our family did too.

I open the cupboard and notice that the cereal box is close to empty. I pull out the milk and don't have enough.

This is just great.

# HINTS

.....

I'm in the garage grabbing the tent, when I stop and think about the purpose of the trip. It'd be better if we just laid out with nothing blocking our view of the stars. So I put the tent back on the shelf.

I'm outside sitting on the cooler, waiting for Seth. Tickles is curled at my feet. My backpack is stocked with stuff.

Susan pulls up in her car, and both she and Seth get out. "You must have some magic power, Charlie. I haven't seen Seth up this early since school ended."

Seth yawns a big, wide, attention-getting yawn. He makes a lot of noise.

"Excited for this, Charlie?" asks Susan. "I made you both some turkey sandwiches—"

"Lots and lots of turkey sandwiches," says Seth.

"I love turkey sandwiches," I say.

"I know," says Seth.

"There's also some chocolate chip cookies—the ones

you liked so much, Charlie—and some potato salad and chips. Oh, and I bought a package of hot dogs and buns. There's also some mustard and ketchup. Did I mention the chips?"

"Basically we're packing the kitchen with us." Seth's camera hangs around his neck.

"Funny," says Susan. "I just want to make sure you're both prepared. This is actually really dangerous. I don't want you boys going too far. Your dad knows, I hope?"

I nod.

"And do you have a first aid kit?"

"Uh." I look at my stuff.

"I have a spare. Seth, can you grab that from the trunk?"

"She means she bought one for us." Seth puts his stuff down on the lawn and goes digging in the trunk of the car.

"I want you two to be safe. Where are you camping, Charlie? Seth didn't seem to know many details."

"Oh, uh, just up that mountain there." I point behind me. "Not too far. Maybe a couple of miles in."

"Two miles in, max. I want you both to be careful. Hear me? Don't do anything stupid." Susan then says quietly, "I can't believe I'm allowing this." She turns to Seth. "Come give me a kiss."

Seth slouches over.

"Charlie, I want a hug from you, too."

As I release the hug, I say, "Oh, can you tell my grandma what I'm doing and that I'll see her later this week?"

"Absolutely. I'll tell her today. Do you boys have your phones?"

We both hold out our phones.

"Of course you do. Seth, I want you to call twice a day. Morning, noon, and night."

"That's three times," he says.

Susan glares at him.

"We might not have reception." I look at all our stuff and back to Susan.

"Well, find some. That's all I ask."

"Okay. Thanks, Mom. Bye."

She nods but stands there a little longer. "Do you boys need anything before I leave?"

"I think we've got it from here," I say.

"Yeah. ALL GOOD, Mom."

Tickles barks. "Well, I think he's ready to get going," I say to Susan more than anyone else.

"Love you both," she says. "Be careful."

*Love you too, Susan.* I stand with my hands in my shorts pockets.

Seth says nothing.

She gets into her Toyota 4Runner and waves. As she drives away, she honks. Seth turns to me. "She's literally suffocating me."

I laugh, and wonder why I no longer feel as angry at Seth as I did last night. Maybe it's because he's still my best friend and we're getting to go alien hunting.

"It's not funny. You don't live with her."

"You say that as if living with her is a bad thing," I say.

"Isn't it?"

"The alternative would be having no one around."

"Oh my god. Sign me up."

"Are we ready?" I ask.

"For a nap? Yes."

"Dream on," I say.

"That's what I'm asking for."

"Ha-ha," I say. "So who's carrying all of this food? There's only two of us."

"That's what I was trying to tell her!"

"It's okay. Deep breaths."

He exaggeratedly takes in deep breaths.

This is going to be fun.

Before we even get to the forest, Seth says, "I'm tired."

"We just started."

There's some silence as we keep walking, except for Tickles's bell ringing, but I even tune that out after a while.

About a mile in, Seth is complaining that his back hurts from the backpack, so we put the cooler down, since we're each holding one side, and sit on it.

I look out to the woods, and I hear a *click*. I turn and see that Seth has taken a picture of me. I pout.

"Didn't you get the memo? I'm the official trip photographer."

"No, the memo didn't come through."

"Oh, darn. I guess you'll just have to put up with me, then." Seth lightheartedly punches me in the arm.

"Ow," I say.

"That didn't hurt."

"Okay, but I wasn't expecting it."

"Expect the unexpected," he says.

"What?"

"That's it. Expect the unexpected. It's really the key to life."

"What are you, a philosopher now?"

"Feel free to bow down to the Great Wise Master."

I stand up and sling the backpack over my shoulder. "How about I kick the Great Wise One?"

"Correction: 'Great Wise Master.' Not 'Great Wise One.'"

"Get your great wise ass up so we can continue."

Seth crosses his arms and pouts. "I don't wanna."

"Suit yourself. You'll have to carry the cooler by yourself, then. Come on, Tickles."

Seth jumps up. "No, no. Fine. I'm ready."

I laugh. "I see that worked." We pick up the cooler and begin walking. "This thing is heavy."

"Those damn turkey sandwiches." Seth grunts.

"So I think we'll have to go more than two miles in. Your mom said—"

"Don't worry about that. She's just a worrier. We have to do right by this trip."

"Are you sure?" I ask.

"How would she know? I'll just tell her what she wants to hear."

"Okay," I say. "Great."

"On second thought," he says, "two miles might be as far as I'm willing to carry this damn thing."

# FOLLOW THROUGH

. . . . .

Pine trees and boulders dot the land. Between the trees
and boulders are tall grasses and sagebrush. Though, as
we keep walking farther and farther into the deep, the
trees are closing in on one another. They're getting harder
to walk through.

"Are we almost there?" asks Seth, winded.

"Why don't we take a break here. Maybe have a turkey
sandwich?"

We lower the cooler. Seth takes off his backpack and
crashes to the ground. "You really don't know how much
farther? Why don't we just stay here?"

"Why are you so tired? We've maybe gone two miles.
Three, tops."

"I'm not much for all this exercise," says Seth jokingly.
He sits up and drinks some water. "How will we know
when we're there?"

"Oh, I'll know the spot."

"Ugh," says Seth. He lies back on the ground.

"Why don't you stop complaining and enjoy the adventure?"

Tickles runs over and sits next to Seth. Seth scratches him behind the ears. "I agree, boy. Charlie is totally torturing us. Yes, I know he's mean. But we can't say anything to him or he'll zap our brains into mush with his alien laser. Shhh! We can't let him know we're onto him."

I unwrap a sandwich. "Really?"

Seth looks around. "Hmmm? Oh, nothing. Nothing. Just enjoying the weather."

I can't help but bust out laughing.

"Throw me one of those sandwiches," he says.

I grab one and am turning back to toss it at Seth, when he takes another picture of me. "You need to stop that."

"Trip photographer. Sorry not sorry."

# THE ONE

·····

Now *my* legs are tired, but I don't tell Seth. We keep trudging on. Deeper and deeper into the woods. Seth's complaining mostly grew quiet after the fourth mile.

The world is so quiet. No distant highway noise, no music, no evidence that humans have ever stepped foot on this land before.

We reach a clearing with nothing but grass, and I stop. Looking around, I announce, "This is it."

"What?" Seth looks up at me, blinking.

"This is the spot."

Seth's eyes spark like a struck match. "Seriously? We made it? Oh my god, I thought we'd never get here. You know? Like I was trapped in one of those circles of hell. 'Wandering,' or whatever it's called." He drops his stuff.

Tickles starts to run over to Seth.

"No, Tickles," I say. "Don't get close. You'll catch Melodrama Fever."

Seth runs in a circle, shouting, "This clearing is too

small! And it's not woody enough to be woods! And the world is ending! Ahh!"

Tickles barks. I boo. "Get off the stage."

"I'm hungry," says Seth, no longer running.

"We have sandwiches."

"I'm already sick of turkey," he says. "Let's do something fun."

"Okay." I wait for a suggestion.

"Oh, uh . . ." Seth looks around. "Hot dogs?"

"We'd have to build a fire."

"Do you know how to do that?"

"Wait. Don't you?"

"I've never been camping before. Remember?"

It really is heretical for someone from Montana to say this, at least out loud. "Weren't you born in Montana?" I ask.

Seth looks at me like I'm offending him. "Yes, Charlie. But not everyone born in Montana likes the same things. And I never really had a chance to go camping. Until now."

"Okay, sorry." I get quiet and wander around, collecting twigs.

Seth comes over to me. "How can I help?"

"Well." I look at the ground. "Can you find some rocks to make a fire ring?"

"Ah? Sure."

"Don't worry. I'll help."

Seth smiles. "I trust you."

Seth is bent over, watching the twigs slowly ignite and the flames grow stronger.

"This is amazing," says Seth once the fire is sufficiently burning.

I add more branches to it.

Seth leans back. "Ouch."

"Don't sit too close."

"How about I sit close to you instead?"

I look at him and then feel awkward again. I'm not sure why I'm having that feeling around Seth lately. Is it me or him?

We're both quiet, but at least the fire is keeping me entertained. Crackling and burning, splitting logs and throwing burning amber and ash into the air, glowing until it burns to nothing.

# POSSIBLE WORLDS IN A
# UNIVERSE SO VAST

.....

Tickles lies next to us in our sleeping bags.

The moon is out and the fire is still burning, but not as strongly. We're neglecting it while we wait and search, talk, and hunt the dark sky.

After some time has passed since we last spoke, Seth asks, "Why do you think we're here?"

"Because we wanted to go camping."

"No." Seth chuckles. "Like, here. On Earth."

"Oh. Uh. The big bang?"

Seth turns to me. "Do you believe in that?"

"You don't?"

"Isn't it weird to think that an explosion caused our being here? Like, we're just the aftermath of some bomb. A collection of debris."

"A collection of debris?" I say. "Doesn't that sound kind of cool? We're basically made up of space rocks. And we can think. And dream. And write. And love. And we're just debris. Don't you think that's amazing?"

"I mean, when you put it that way. But what about God? Adam and Eve?"

"What about them?"

Seth shakes his head. "So you're not a religious person, I take it?"

"I don't know. If there's a God, then I'm convinced he's made out of space dust too."

"I was raised Catholic."

"I wasn't raised anything in particular."

There's silence between us as the stars in the far galaxies twinkle and shine and freeze and burn and make other space rock people.

"Isn't the universe amazing?" I ask. "Like, just so vast?" I enjoy the time looking up, right into the sky. No screen around. Almost like there's a direct connection between the universe above and me below it all. This is time I spend contemplating my life, and the Big Questions.

Seth looks up and watches the sky with me, but doesn't say anything.

"There is something like a hundred billion galaxies in the universe. Like, not planets or stars, but galaxies with all their own planets and stars." I take a deep breath, letting the enormity of the universe settle in on my chest. Seth remains silent. Reflective, perhaps. "Sometimes I think I like looking up because I realize how small I really am. See that star? None of my problems matter to that gigantic star. Or all those stars that make up the Big Dipper? They don't care what I'm going through. In fact, they don't even know of my existence. Or care. I am nothing to everything beyond me."

"That seems depressing."

"I guess it could be depressing. But also kind of freeing, you know? Like, nothing I ever do will matter to those stars. To our own star. Probably not even to our Earth."

"So what's the point of even being alive?" asks Seth.

I shrug, but I don't think he can see that. "What's the point of anything?"

Seth smirks. "What kind of answer is that?"

"A truthful one."

After a few seconds Seth asks, "So we're looking for UFOs?"

"I think that's one reason why I want to be taken by aliens. Because then maybe I would matter. I would matter to something out there. Some planet in the Great Beyond. Because I would matter to the aliens on that planet."

"By that logic, you matter to Earth."

I keep looking up. "How's that?"

"Because if you matter to humans, then you matter to Earth. And you matter to me."

"That's not exactly what I mean."

"Well, that's what you said. Oh, and by the way," says Seth. "You said it was freeing not to matter to anything, but then you said you wanted to matter to something. Make up your damn mind."

"Well, I mean—" Crap. I don't know what I mean. Maybe all this talk is nothing but talk. Maybe I want both? To be free and to matter. Does that even make any sense?

And then I hear what Seth just said: "You matter to me." It echoes around in my head.

And the earth keeps spinning while the stars stay glued to the sky. And I stay glued to the stars.

You matter to me.

\* \* \*

The night entrenches itself more deeply into darkness as Seth and I stay in our sleeping bags. The fire is nothing but tiny flames though still providing some light. I purposely keep the fire small so that we can still see the sky.

Seth yawns. "So we're just supposed to stare at the sky for another four hours?"

"Yep. All night."

"You know what would suck?"

"Huh?"

"If we stayed up all night, and then the moment we fell asleep, at like six this morning, the sky lit up with UFOs." Seth laughs.

"Okay, jerk. Why would you even say that? Now I'm never going to sleep. Ever again."

Seth laughs more. "Sorry. That was kind of mean."

I keep quiet, even though I feel like I should say something.

"I'm sure we'd hear or see something, right?" asks Seth. "We'd be woken up."

"Tell me more about the light you saw."

"Uh. What do you want to know?"

"Anything. I want to know if it was the same light as I saw. Maybe the same UFO?" I turn and rest on my forearm. "Can I tell you a secret? They're looking for me."

Seth doesn't say anything right away, and I instantly regret what I said. The feeling of stupidity begins to swallow me.

"I already know you think that," he says. "But I can't figure out why you think that."

In the light from the flickering fire, I can see his

face—his eyes as they're boring holes into my own. He's looking at me as if I'm an alien. "Because my mom told me."

There were a lot of doors slammed that night. It felt like ten people were living in our house. My parents were doing a lot of yelling, which I could hear in my bedroom even though my music was playing.

It was dark outside.

It was a school night.

I had just gotten into bed and turned off my lamp, when my bedroom door opened and in walked my mom. She sat on the edge of my bed and didn't say a word. She just combed my hair with her fingers.

"Mom? Are you and Dad getting a divorce?"

She laughed. "No, honey. We're not getting a divorce."

"Okay. Good."

"But the aliens . . . they spoke to me again. They're coming, Charlie. I'm close to leaving. So very close."

"But you can't leave me."

"They are giving me no choice. But I talked with them."

I sat up. "What did they say?"

"They want me now. But they'll come for you later."

"Me later?"

She nodded, kissed me on the forehead, and as she went away said, "Later."

When I woke up the next morning, the house was empty. I figured my dad had left early for work, like normal. But my mom should've been around. She was always around in the mornings. But that morning she was gone. And I haven't seen her since.

* * *

"Your mom is now with the aliens?" asks Seth.

"Yeah."

"I don't know, Charlie. This is a little weird. You really think your mom was abducted by aliens? Seriously?"

"She's gone. And she predicted it. Besides, there are a lot of aliens out there in the Great Beyond. There's probably more alien species than animal species on Earth. And that's like millions. And you even saw a light and heard a loud noise yourself. I mean, what else could that be?"

Side note: I know there are many things it *could* be—and they would make more sense than it having something to do with aliens. But I refuse to lose hope. You can think yourself out of everything magical in life. And what's the point of a life without the possibility of something magical happening? Maybe that's what I should've said to Seth when he asked about the point of being here.

I look at the twinkling stars—and steady my gaze. I am ready, more than ready, to see something out there.

"I made it up," Seth says.

"Made what up?"

"The light. The noise. I'm sorry, Charlie. I just wanted to—"

"You made it up?" I'm oddly not even mad. I'm more sad, this feels like a betrayal from a person I trusted. "Why would you do that?" I push out of my small, confining sleeping bag and walk toward the edge of the clearing.

"Charlie? Where are you going?"

But I keep going.

"Charlie? Stop and let me explain."

I hear footsteps on the forest floor of dry pine needles, rocks, and twigs. So I pick up my pace.

"Charlie. Stop!"

I don't stop until I reach a large boulder and climb up on top of it, my mind a mess of swirling thoughts: aliens-stars-universe-Seth-light-noise-sad-Mom. I stand, looking out across the forest. With the moonlight so strong, I can see the valley and treetops down below. I can see the larger, more intimidating mountain range in the distance. I can see everything. I even see Seth climbing up the rock.

Seth finishes climbing up and sits. "I am seriously out of breath."

"You betrayed my trust, Seth."

"I thought this alien stuff was like a hobby or something. And I thought you kind of knew none of this was real."

"This is all real! I spend my life searching—and looking—and wondering, and that's real to me."

Seth stares at me. He looks hurt. "Can I be honest?"

I can't even nod to him. I stand there, arms crossed.

"I was worried that night after we went swimming. You just seemed so cold and distant to me. Especially on the bike ride home—you didn't even talk. It was like you didn't want to be anywhere near me. And that night before, at Jennifer's, you were so mad at me and ignored all my phone calls. I panicked. I was worried that you might not talk to me again. So I made the UFO thing up, hoping that you'd still talk to me. That you'd still . . . be my friend."

"Yeah, well . . ."

"I know it was stupid. I'm sorry. But can you at least see why I panicked?"

Even though I don't want to say anything to make him feel better, because I somehow feel so hurt, I say, "Maybe."

"I'll take a maybe."

I wonder if I should bring it up. I dig my foot into the dirt and then decide to go for it. "While we're on the subject of Jennifer Bennett, I'd love to know what is going on between you and her."

"What do you mean?"

"You know I like her. You knew that the first time we walked down the school hallway together. So, are you trying to steal her?"

"Really? Really, Charlie? You know, for someone who's always looking, you can be so completely blind. You can't see things standing right in front of you, because you're too busy staring up. And I hate to say it, but life isn't above us. It's in front of us. And maybe it's time you pay attention to what's in front of you."

"What are you talking about?"

"What do you think? Is that why you've been so mad?" Seth laughs to himself, like he suddenly gets it. "It is, isn't it? You think I've been trying to steal Jennifer Bennett away from you."

The way Seth is talking makes me feel like I was being an idiot. But I just listen.

"I'm not trying to steal Jennifer Bennett from you, Charlie."

I muster up the strength to say, "It sure seems that way. Like that night when you were in her room forev—"

"No, Charlie. I'm gay."

# SHATTERINGS

•••••

Immediately after Seth's words are absorbed into the universe, I feel like the world's biggest dick. How could I not have known that? Or maybe I did know, but the thought scared me. Scared me for what it meant for our friendship.

Seth turns to me. "Charlie, I'm a mess. I'm in love with someone who can't even see me."

"So . . . you're not in love with Jennifer Bennett?"

"Oh my god. No. I'm not. Never have been. She's, you know, not my type."

Tickles, tied up by the sleeping bags, barks in the distance.

"So who are you in love with?"

Seth laughs.

"What's so funny?" But he won't stop laughing. "Seriously. I'm trying to help."

He quiets down and looks up at the stars. "Let's just say he's the world's most oblivious person."

I'm starting to think that it might be me . . . but it

couldn't be. Right? So I ask, "Do I know him? Is he gay?"

"I'm not sure you've ever actually met."

"Does he live—"

"And as far as your second question, I'm not sure." He stares into my eyes. "Are you?"

I find myself leaning back. "Me? What? You're . . . with me?" Maybe I'm overreacting because I don't want him to think I've suspected anything. But I think I have suspected. But that doesn't erase the shock when hearing it confirmed.

I find myself hoping that a UFO will appear right now, if only so I can be taken to a world where shame and embarrassment don't exist.

"Dumb, right?" says Seth.

His words hurt me. I don't like the pain I've caused my best friend. No, it's not dumb. I mean, yeah, kind of dumb, because I have never given Seth a reason to believe I'm gay. Have I?

Am I?

Do I like Seth as more than a friend? Do I even know what that would feel like? And what about Jennifer Bennett? I thought I liked her, too. But I feel so much closer to Seth.

Frankly, I spent so long without a friend that the thought of anything more has never crossed my mind. This is all a big mess that I've caused. I clearly suck at being a friend.

"You really think I'm gay?" I ask.

Seth leans back. "Charlie, don't."

"Don't what?"

"Make me answer that."

The only girl I've ever liked, or found truly attractive, is Jennifer Bennett. A girl so far out of my league that it might as well be a fantasy. A girl I can't bring myself to talk to. Do I like her only because she was the most human person at that school?

Did I ever have a chance with her?

Could I still have a chance? It could be like in one of those movies where the dorky guy gets the hot girl. That happens in real life, right?

Somehow thinking through my situation with Jennifer Bennett, knowing that my chances with her were never based in reality, is kind of a revelation to me. Even somewhat freeing.

"Can we just forget that this conversation ever happened?" asks Seth, and I see his eyes glisten in the moonlight.

But the more I let his words sink in, the more I feel that they're drilling a hole into my soul, shattering some kind of wall.

"I don't think so," I say. "I think this is a pivotal moment in our friendship. And I see two options—one will allow us to become the bestest of friends, and the other will destroy our friendship. We need to proceed cautiously."

I jump down from the boulder and put up my hand like it's a gun at the ready. I'm like a spy getting ready to bust into a building. Except I'm not. At all.

"Where are you going?"

"Proceeding cautiously." I walk a few feet and turn to Seth, who's watching me quizzically from the rock. "Well, come on." I keep the hand gun at the ready.

Seth jumps down off the rock. "Charlie. This is

ridiculous. I feel like an idiot. I just want to go back to my sleeping bag."

"Nonsense." I'm walking farther away from the sleeping bags.

"What are you doing with your hands? What is going on? I literally just told you I'm gay, and now you're acting weird."

It's true—I have no idea what I'm doing. I think I just want to make Seth laugh. I want to make him forget about all this, but I'm acting like too big a weirdo and am probably just creeping him out.

"They're just right over that hill, Captain." I slowly sneak like the spy I'm not. I even get down onto my knees and slowly move toward a fallen tree. When I turn back, I see Seth walking back to the sleeping bags.

Shit.

# SEEING

·····

As I follow Seth from a distance, I begin to think that he might be the only person who actually sees me. It's an interesting thought to have, and maybe it has something to do with his being a photographer? His life is all about catching moments that others miss, finding those quiet and unobtrusive slices of life on a busy city street; or seeing those loud, unignorable cracks in a person that the person can't see in himself.

But I also think Seth sees me in ways that aren't visible to the eye, a way of seeing that requires truly listening, and being attentive, and stepping away from one's own fleeting yet constant needs, in order to actually be there for someone else. Maybe I'm reading way too much into this, and I just feel terrible for not seeing Seth in a deeper, more meaningful way. How could I be so blind?

Seth walks in front of me with his head down. I don't even know how to begin to salvage our friendship. I really messed things up.

We get into our sleeping bags, and I move around for a few seconds, listening to the nylon scratching.

"Tell me more about you," I say.

"It's okay, Charlie. I think I might just get some sleep." Seth turns away from me and lies on his side.

Normally I don't mind the silence, especially in the woods, but when I think about Seth no longer awake, anxiety washes over me. I am so small against the backdrop of the sky, and Seth is turned away from me. I am neglected, and it's my own doing.

"Please don't sleep," I whisper.

"What?"

"I'd really love to know," I say.

An occasional wheeze comes from Tickles as he sleeps away. Sometimes I'm jealous of animals who seem to be able to sleep no matter what is crumbling around them.

"It's just . . . I think you're only asking because you feel guilty. Because I brought it up. Not because you want to know."

I put my hand on his cool shoulder. "I really want to know. We're best friends, aren't we?"

Seth is quiet a moment. He turns to face me and stares intently into my eyes. "Okay. Fine. What do you want to know?"

"Whatever you want to tell me."

"Do you want to know why we're in Whitehall? Why I showed up three weeks before school ended?"

I nod. "Only ever since you arrived."

"My mom didn't think Miles City was safe anymore."

"What do you mean?"

"Well, without sounding too melodramatic, word got

out that I was gay. . . . Long story about that. But basically I was dating the mayor's son, and he wasn't out, and anyway . . ." Seth shakes his head. "It's kind of funny. So I start getting mysterious death threats. . . . I'm pretty sure Josh organized them. The mayor's son. And they were freaking my mom out, but I figured they were mostly just scare tactics. But one day I went outside to leave for school and saw the words 'death to faggots' spray-painted on our garage door."

"Jesus." I can barely believe what I'm hearing.

"So my mom packed us up and we headed for the first place she found a job."

"Whitehall."

"Whitehall," Seth repeats. "I kept trying to tell her that if we were already moving, we might as well go somewhere cool like Portland or Seattle. But she isn't so keen on big cities."

"I had no idea."

Seth is quiet. "It's not something I really enjoy sharing."

I don't know what to say. I'm literally in shock. "Who would do such a thing?"

Seth shrugs. "Someone who hates himself? I think I'm going to take some pictures."

"But it's dark out."

"So it is." Seth gets out of his sleeping bag and rifles through his backpack until he pulls out a camera case and a tripod.

Next to our sleeping bags he sets up his tripod and mounts his camera, before pointing it up to the sky. "You can get some really cool shots at night. Like, long-exposure stuff can even bring out the Milky Way."

"Really?"

"Yeah. Haven't you seen any of those kind of pictures? They're all over online."

"I'll have to look."

"I'll show you one tonight—if I capture a good one. Actually, the camera can pick up things that the human eye would normally miss."

"Seriously? So there could be a UFO right in front of us and we might not see it, but the camera would?" I say, getting out of my sleeping bag.

"I mean, probably not. But you never know."

I stand, looking up at the sky. I almost can't believe that a UFO could be right in front of my eyes, but then again, I can totally believe it. "Take a picture."

"That's what I'm working on."

"No, like a quick snap, so we can see if there's anything above us right now."

"Well, it doesn't quite work like that."

"Oh. Well, how does it work?"

"Let me just take a long exposure, and we can see what we see."

Seth adjusts the camera; he looks into the eye-hole thing. I don't know what it's called. I go pet Tickles and then untie him from the tree. I'm walking in circles with Tickles and occasionally stealing glances at Seth. The night gets longer. I pet Tickles again.

"Come look," Seth finally says.

Looking at the screen on the back of the camera, I see a still shot of a ton of stars. And I can kind of see the Milky Way snaking its way through the center. I see lots of colors in the shot that I don't see when I look up. Like purples and blues. But I don't see the one thing I'm looking for.

"That's an amazing photo."

"Thanks," says Seth, who looks at me and lingers a moment too long before turning back to his camera. "I'm going to try another one."

His second shot is even better. It has deeper, more vibrant colors, and it has a better something . . . Seth calls it composition. But honestly, I think both shots are amazing, and as we are looking at his second picture on his camera, I see out of the corner of my eye a great flash. It is about as quick as a photo snap, but leaves a longer impression.

We both duck as it seems to buzz the tops of the trees, but it's gone before either of us can get a good look at it.

Everything happens so quickly, and there is no crash landing, because we don't hear anything, don't see any debris or dust. In fact, it's like nothing happened at all.

Except it did.

"What was that?" Seth asks, breathless. His eyes look wild. "Was it a shooting star? It was super, super close. We should be dead right now."

I turn to him, my heart racing; I'm more nervous than I ever thought I'd be at this point. I'm almost frightened. "They're here."

Seth nervously asks, "Who's here?"

"The aliens."

And that's when Tickles takes off into the woods.

# WANDER TO THE EDGE

·····

"Grab your camera!" I scream as we both run after Tickles—and maybe we're more chasing whatever that thing was that just practically grazed our heads. Well, I am.

I sense that my mom is close, and I can't help my excitement.

We're heading in the right direction, but I don't hear Tickles. I'm worried about losing Geoffrey's dog, but in all honesty, I probably won't see Geoffrey again. I realize that's a mean thought, and I kind of hate myself for thinking it.

Up ahead Tickles barks, and I pick up my pace.

"Tickles, stop running!"

Seth is right behind me. But every time I look back, he's getting farther behind.

"Come on! Keep up!"

"I am," he says, out of breath.

When I get to the top of the hill, I stop running and

look around. I hear Seth closing in. Soon he's next to me, breathing hard, but I can't hear anything else. I can't see anything either.

Son of a bitch.

There's no dog.

There's no UFO.

There's nothing but forest stretching for miles and miles under the tutelage of moonlight.

"Ugh."

"What's wrong?" asks Seth

Moving away from Seth, I shout, "I'm here! I'm up here! Come on, please don't leave me!"

I turn, and Seth's expression says it all. He looks hurt. Sad.

Seth kicks at the ground, and his mood seems sour. "So you could leave? Just like that?"

And that's when it hits me: if I go with the aliens, then I'll be leaving my best friend. I'll be leaving him like my parents left me. And that thought feels awful.

And that awful feeling bothers the shit out of me.

I have to play dumb, because the more I think about it, the less I know what I'd do. "What are you talking about? I'm right here."

He shakes his head angrily. "No. With these aliens. If they wanted to take you, you wouldn't put up a fight? You'd just go with them?"

"Sure." But I'm not so sure now.

"That's fucked."

It's not fucked. It's survival. "You wouldn't?"

"No way. I have an amazing life to live here, on this planet. I hope to teach photography at some amazing art school in New York and have this hugely fulfilling career shooting for presidents and magazines and art galleries. I'll have my own dog. And kids. I'm even going to get married someday."

I let his dreams sink in. That all sounds amazing for Seth, but those aren't my dreams.

"Do you?" Seth asks.

"Do I what?" I ask, confused.

"Do you have any dreams, Charlie? Besides this UFO thing? Do you have any wants or goals or aspirations in this life?"

My mind is blank. I haven't had anyone in my family aspire to much, and my life is pretty much shit. My mom disappeared and my grandma doesn't know I exist and I get bullied at school and my friend Geoffrey might be eating himself to death and Tickles has only three legs and we still don't know who hit him and no one in my family has ever asked me, "Charlie, what are your dreams?" And now my dad has seemingly left me as well. Oh, and Seth seems pretty much done with me at this point too. I really can't do anything right, and I'm sick of trying. So, dreams? No, I haven't thought about a dream that doesn't include me being taken to somewhere far from Whitehall and Montana and this earth.

"Yes. I have dreams."

Seth wills me to continue.

"Um, I want to—"

I search my mind. My thoughts. My past. Fragments of my life pass before my eyes. My mom. My tricycle. Cooking with my grandma. My parents fighting. Geoffrey moving next door. Tickles peeing on me. Flying nowhere but in my mind. That's when it hits me.

"Fly."

"What?"

I clear my throat. "A pilot. I want to be a plane pilot." And just like that I suddenly do. I want to fly. I want to be up in the sky. It's the best of all worlds—up above this one, but still connected to the earth—to the people that make life matter.

Seth's eyes seem to light up. "Really? I had no idea, Charlie."

Me either. I don't know how I didn't piece this puzzle together before. "Yeah. A pilot."

I turn back out to the darkened forest and search for the lost dog and the lost UFO and everything I've worked for. Everything I've searched for. Even when I'm already in the woods, I can't find the damn UFO. I'm a failure, and it feels like the aliens don't want me to find them. If they did, why would they make it so hard?

Seth studies me and, apparently seeing my despair, sits cross-legged, on the ground.

I throw up my hands. "Now what are you doing? We need to get the dog."

Seth doesn't say anything, and the next thing I know, he has his camera up to his eye. *Snap.* He takes a picture of me.

"This isn't the time to take—"

*Snap.*

"Seriously, Seth. Stop—"

*Snap.*

"Stop!"

I hear his camera click again, capturing me in a range of emotions and looks, and I'm not comfortable with any of it.

"You're alive," he finally says. "You know that?"

"Duh," I say. "Of course I'm alive."

The camera clicks again.

Out of desperation, I turn my back to him.

"See, you say that, but I don't think you really believe it."

"Why do you say that?" My back is still to him.

I hear the scraping of dirt as he gets up and stands right behind me.

"Because you act like your life hasn't begun. You always talk about these aliens as if your life would officially start once they take you. But how do you know your life wouldn't stop? I'm sorry for what I'm about to say, but how do you even know your mom is alive? If she was really taken by aliens, like you say, then what's to say she—"

"Don't."

"Isn't being tortured?"

"Stop it."

"Or being used for some messed up experiment where they've sawed off her arms and legs and she's a type of robot?"

"Please!"

"Or that she's just . . . dead."

I turn to face him, the tears streaming down my face. "Why would you say that?"

Seth hugs me tightly. He squeezes out all the air between us. It's just us in the universe at this moment.

A moment.

Then my pocket vibrates. I accidentally left my phone on. I pull it out and see that I have a bit of service—and notice that I have a voice mail from an unknown number.

I put my phone up to my ear. "Hey, Charlie. This is

Ted, your dad's friend. We went to your house, but you weren't home. And it's taken us a little while to find your number. . . . I have a bit of bad news."

My heart stops beating as I hold my breath.

"Your dad went fishing with us, and he wanted to go for a hike yesterday to get some cell service and call you . . . but we started getting worried when he didn't come back after a few hours. By late last night he had been gone for the better part of the day. Anyway, Charlie, we're gathering up some men, and the sheriff is out trying to find him. I'm sure he's safe, and maybe just got turned around. When you get this, give me a call back."

I slowly lower the phone as the words sink in.

"What's wrong?" asks Seth.

"My dad. He's missing."

# DREAMS IN SHADOWS

· · · · ·

In the blackness I hear a bark. That's encouraging. And then more barks. I need to get Tickles. But I also need to go find my dad.

And then I remember the UFO that has to be so close and yet feels so far away. But that's okay. The UFO, for once, can be far away.

"Tickles!" I shout. "Come here, boy."

"Tickles!" shouts Seth.

The trees are thicker around us, letting less moonlight through, so I pull out my phone and turn on the flashlight. "Tickles!"

The forest is quiet.

"He last barked in this direction." I point down the hill to the west. We briskly walk down the hill. "We absolutely cannot lose him. Geoffrey would never forgive me."

It strikes me that I'm thinking about Geoffrey's reaction. It's like I'm not leaving now, and I'm not upset by that thought.

Tickles's barking gets louder, and I pick up my pace, moving quickly over rocks and fallen trees in the dark.

"I think he's close," I shout, but I see Seth falling farther behind again. Right after I say that, the barking stops. I keep going in the same direction until the next bark I hear sounds like it's coming from behind me. I turn around. The next bark I hear sounds like it's coming from my left side. The next bark sounds like it's from my right side. It feels like I'm surrounded on all sides by dogs. . . . I feel dizzy and I lose my footing, and my leg slides out from under me and I fall, and my head smacks the ground. Hard.

"Charlie!" I hear. But I don't see Seth.

"I'm okay," I say, standing up. My head throbs with every heartbeat. The barking continues on all sides and grows louder.

I feel disoriented. Through the barking I hear Seth's words in my head, questioning whether my mother was tortured, or is perhaps dead. And suddenly I'm scared. I don't like this. I don't want to be abducted. I don't want to die.

Five mangy, rabid-looking wolves emerge from the darkened trees and are coming toward me from all sides. As they draw closer, they begin to stand on two legs, their fur tearing apart as if it were nothing but fake skin, a costume. But they still have their fangs and claws. There's some kind of translucent skin underneath the wolf fur that now hangs from their bodies. Their eyes are small and sharp-looking. And yellow.

Next thing I know, just like with Meridian X, I can't move my arms or legs or even my mouth. I'm stuck.

I see the fangs of the alien in front of me. I'd shiver

if I could move. The alien takes a claw and slowly cuts horizontally across the top part of my forehead. I feel the warm blood running down the bridge of my nose. Another alien pulls open the skin, and I see him place a thin chip-like device into my forehead. Their breath is cold on my skin.

As quickly as they appeared, they disappear. My mind goes black, and soon I am staring into the eyes of Seth as he hovers over me.

"Oh, thank god," he says. "You're awake."

I lean up and look around. "What happened?"

"You tripped and hit your head on that rock pretty hard."

I touch my forehead, which is bleeding. I quickly look up, and there appears to be nothing there. I look around. "Was anyone else here? Five wolflike creature things?"

Seth looks at me strangely. "Uh . . . just us. You must've really hit your head. Maybe you should rest in case you got a concussion."

"I'm fine," I say, standing up. "Where's Tickles?"

"I heard him barking just up on that ridge over there."

"Let's go get him. Maybe you can lead this time?"

Seth smiles and starts walking. As I follow, I touch my cut, feeling for anything chip-like inside.

We are close to the top of the ridge, and Tickles is sitting there, almost like he's been patiently waiting here the entire time. He barks as we get close. "Tickles," I say. "You bad dog."

"Charlie? Do you know where we are? Or how to get back?"

"Nope. But . . ." I look up to the sky. "Follow me."

\* \* \*

We walk through the pine trees, around the boulders, dog on leash, Seth next to me. I'm oddly serene. Though, I shouldn't be. After all, my dad is officially missing. I don't know for sure if I was just chipped by aliens, which means I might be missing soon myself.

Seth and I are silent. Both in our heads.

"Do you think your dad has been abducted?" Seth asks.

I hear twigs crunch as we walk toward the campsite. Seth's words are heavy. Doused with something like truth. My dad has been abducted—his soul was taken by my mom, when she left. He has never been the same.

"I mean, he was in the woods when he disappeared."

"Lots of people are in the woods when they disappear," I say.

"So you don't think he was abducted?"

I shake my head. "Doubtful. He probably got drunk and got lost."

Seth stops walking. "Charlie? Is that you?"

I walk a few more feet and turn back to him.

"The Charlie I know would be swearing up and down that his father was abducted by aliens."

I shrug. "I guess I don't really believe he was abducted."

We keep walking, letting the silence wash back over us.

I realize that I gotta get out of the woods. I gotta get home. I gotta find my dad.

But knowing that Seth is near me makes me feel, I don't know, okay about life.

# LONG NIGHT LOOKING HOME

. . . . .

The ground crunches beneath our feet, and I'm holding Tickles because he got smart and stopped walking a few yards back. Even though he got us here in the first place.

"How do you know how to get back to our sleeping bags?" asks Seth.

"Polaris."

"Huh?"

"The North Star."

"Okay?"

"Polaris is another name for the North Star, which happens to be right above the North Pole. So I found that. If you face it, you're looking due north. I know we ran north, so we just had to turn and go south."

"But doesn't the earth always spin? Aren't the constellations always changing?"

"Yeah, but the North Star remains fairly fixed. At least up here in Montana. It actually has been known as the Wanderer's Star because it acts as a sort of compass. It's almost like an anchor for the northern sky to spin around."

"An anchor?" Seth laughs.

"What?"

"Even the sky needs an anchor."

"Now I'm confused."

"It's nothing. Just proves a personal theory of mine that everything needs something to ground it."

I turn and look at him. I still don't understand what he's talking about. But I also feel some sort of energy between Seth and me. I can't explain it other than to say that we just went through what felt like a harrowing experience. There's a growing history between us, and I like that.

I want to create more history with Seth. Go on more adventures.

"You know a lot about the sky," he says.

I smile, because I do. I sure do.


It's almost morning by the time we reach the sleeping bags, and I'm tired. My head hurts. All I can think about is sleep.

Seth says, "Should we pack so you can get back to Whitehall?"

"Ugh. I guess. Even though I feel so tired."

We both pack our stuff up in the dark. Tickles on his leash tied to the nearby tree lies down to sleep, and I feel so jealous. But I need to get back home so that I can help look for my dad.

"Ready?" asks Seth.

I'm looking up at the stars as they are ever-so-slowly disappearing into the sky.

"Charlie?"

A week of never ending nights down to two. Then down to not even one. Yet we saw aliens. Right? I believe that I accomplished what I set out to do. Except I'm still here, on Earth, but I think that's good.

"Earth to Charlie?"

I break my gaze with the stars and look at Seth standing in front of me. I smile and look him in the eyes. "I'm here."

As we walk back toward town, we're relatively quiet. We're both exhausted and ready for sleep, but that seems like a long way off.

I catch a blinking red light far out in the sky. My head feels like it's pulsating with the light. It blinks. One. Two. One. Two. Gone.

"There's the Big Dipper. I can find that," says Seth, pointing.

I chuckle. "A regular astronomer."

"Basically I'm a new age Galileo. Isn't that the astronomer guy?"

"No. Different guy."

"Oh. Really? Who am I thinking of?"

I can't hold it in anymore, and bust out a big smile.

"You're messing with me?" He fakes a shocked and appalled look.

"I would never," I say in an exaggerated way.

We've been walking for a few more seconds when the thought that's been bothering me for some time, and especially tonight, comes out, "I'm sorry I've been a shitty friend."

"You're not a shitty friend, Charlie." It feels like the

conversation is over, but then he says, "I am."

Now I'm shocked and appalled for real. I don't even know why he'd ever say that. "No, you're not."

"No, I am. At first, I only wanted to be your friend because I thought you were super cute. And possibly gay."

I think about his reasons. "Okay, yeah, you're a shitty friend."

Seth laughs, and then says, "But I'm glad we're real friends now."

I'm quiet a moment. My thoughts are no clearer on some things, but I do know one thing for sure. "I'm glad we're real friends too."

The crack of hazy blue daylight is opening wider by the minute now. The air feels electrified with the coming day.

"Crazy," says Seth.

"What?"

"It's another day already. Feels like last night was kind of a dream, doesn't it?"

I nod. "Feels like that."

"But a good dream," says Seth. "One for the books."

"One for the books," I repeat.

# A REQUEST (FROM THE HEART)

· · · · ·

My house looms in front of us as we leave the woods, and looking at it, my perspective changes. My house looks . . . different. It's like it doesn't have as much power over me as before. Like it no longer has the power to bring me down. I have no idea why I feel this difference. Maybe because I'm officially the man of the house (at least until my dad gets back). Or maybe it's because of the night I just had with Seth. One thing is certain, I don't want my house and room to ever feel like a tomb again.

I call Ted, my dad's friend, and he says, "Charlie? That you?"

"What's happening, Ted? Where's my dad?"

"Charlie, jeez, been trying to get a hold of you all night. Look. This here's hard to say."

"I already know he's missing."

Seth stares at me as we walk. He holds Tickles's leash.

"It's not that, Charlie."

My stomach drops, and I hold my breath.

"We called the sheriff yesterday. A big search party went out, combed the area, and we found your dad."

"Oh my god, he's dead?"

Seth drops his side of the cooler.

"What?" Ted says. "No. No. But he's mighty injured. Fell a ways off a cliff. Broke a leg, some ribs, shattered his kneecap. Done some other things too."

"Where is he?"

"He's at Memorial. Room eighteen."

I hang up before Ted can say anything else. Seth looks at me with wide eyes. "What's going on?"

"He's at the hospital. They found him. But he's injured."

"I'll bring Tickles back if you want to go?"

"It's fine. Geoffrey's house is literally right there."

We drop off the camping supplies in the garage and head to Geoffrey's. I knock quickly and we enter. Geoffrey is snoring loudly on the couch.

My forehead is pulsating again. I press my finger to it. I can't feel anything.

"Geoffrey," I say loudly.

He keeps snoring.

I let Tickles off the leash. He runs his little legs to the kitchen.

"I'll have to come back," I say, and head out the door. Seth follows me out.

"I'll call you later to see how your dad is doing," he says.

This stops me in my tracks. "You're not coming with me?"

"Maybe it should just be you and your dad."

The thought of being alone, without Seth, digs a pit

into my chest. I hate the empty feeling. And I both hate and love that I need Seth in my life right now. "Can you please come?"

"I've never met your dad."

"You can meet him now."

"Why do you want me to go so badly?"

I shake my head. "Because." *Because you make me feel connected to the ground. Maybe you're my anchor.* "Just . . . come on."

# A
# FALLING
# STAR

. . . . .

For the first time in weeks, my dad is home. He'd been lost
in the woods. He'd been stuck at the hospital. But now he's
situated in his bed.

Ted is the last friend still in the house. He pats my dad's
shoulder. "Glad to get you out of there. I'll check on you
tomorrow."

"Thanks, Ted."

"Charlie, you need anything?" Ted asks.

"I'm good."

The front door closes and we're alone. No friends. No
Seth. No nurses or doctors.

"You look tired," I say, standing by his bedroom door.
"Why don't you get some sleep?"

"Charlie?"

I stand there looking at him.

"I've been doing a lot of thinking lately. You've been
mad ever since your mom left."

"That's not true."

"You're mad at me. You're mad at your mother. And I think you're mad at yourself."

I shake my head. "What are you talking about? I'm not mad. I know she's out there. And she's coming back. Someday. Her and—" Shit. I didn't want to go there with my dad.

"And? Aliens? Is that what you were going to say?" My dad shakes his head with his jaw clenched. "Charlie Dickens, you're a stubborn pain in my ass. You're going to be a sophomore in a few short weeks. It's time you grow up. And accept the truth."

"I know the truth. Mom was targeted by—"

"Enough!" My dad scoots himself up in his bed. "Enough of this bullshit, Charlie. You know your mom wasn't abducted by aliens. You know it. Your mom had—has—some major issues. But she wasn't taken. Look me in the eye and tell me that much. She left us. She did."

"No. Not by choice."

"It was only her choice. I let this alien thing go on for a while because I thought it was some weird coping thing. But it's gotten out of hand—it has been out of hand for some time, and that's my fault. I think you truly believe your mother was taken by aliens, and that scares me, because she truly believed they were coming for her."

"I need to go."

"No, you need to listen to me. I've kept this from you because I didn't see the point in sharing it—especially after she left. And she never wanted you to know—"

"What?"

"Your mother is schizophrenic. She was told that by

a doctor shortly before she left us. Now she's in Indiana. With her mother."

Schizophrenic? What in the actual fuck is he talking about?

"Your mother left us in the middle of the night, Charlie, and I can only assume she kissed you good-bye; for her sake I hope she did. But she didn't so much as come near me."

"This doesn't make any sense."

"I was hoping you'd leave the past behind you and move on—forget the nonsense, especially when you started high school. But I don't think that's working. So grab my phone."

"Why?"

"Come on." He holds out his hand. I walk over to his nightstand and hand him his phone. He types something and presses send. "Check your phone. Maybe it'd do you good to call that number."

"I gotta go." I close the door to my dad's room and run outside to stare at the sky. It's the only thing I think I know.

What the hell is my dad talking about?

I want to quickly forget that entire conversation, except I don't think I can.

# PART FOUR

## A VAST NEW WORLD
## JUST WEST OF MYSELF

# A QUIET SUNDAY

· · · · ·

This is not how I expected to spend my first weekend after school started. But here we are.

Here's the setup: The phone rang. The phone rang again. And again. And though I could kind of hear it in my state between sleep and consciousness, it didn't wake me up until call four or five. My eyes pop open, and I run downstairs in my boxers and answer the landline phone. "Hello?"

After I hear the news, I rush into my dad's room. He's snoring, and his cast-wearing legs are above the covers; I try waking him, but he keeps snoring. I look at his nightstand and see an open bottle of pain pills.

"Dad." I shake him. "We need to go. Now."

More snores.

I stand there wondering what to do. Dump water on him? No, he'd kill me.

I yell, "Dad!" But it's like his mind is somewhere else. Only his body is present.

I don't have time for this, so I run back up to my room,

put on clothes, and head outside. I take my dad's keys and drive his car to the nursing home.

The streets are deserted in Whitehall at five a.m.

This morning's sky: I call this painting *Heaven's Gate and the Accompanying Golden Rods Embracing Another Beautiful Soul.*

The nurse on duty is a guy I've never met. Probably because he only works the night shift and I'm never there at night.

"Where's your dad?" he asks.

I race past him. "Coming."

I get to Grandma's room, and there's nothing wrong with her. She's sleeping and her breath is soft and peaceful.

The nurse is right behind me. I turn to him. "What do you mean she's dying? She seems fine to me. She's sleeping!"

"Sir, calm down. Just wait."

Sure enough, after a moment she stops breathing for a period of ten seconds. "Oh my god. Grandma? Grandma? Is she dead?"

Right then she takes another breath.

"I'll leave you two alone." The nurse walks out.

Her following breaths are irregular. Every time she stops breathing for anywhere between five and fifteen seconds, I find myself holding my own breath. This couldn't be more torturous, because I don't know when her nonbreathing will hold out, that one time when there'll be no more in-breaths.

I look upon my grandma's body. I'm sure she doesn't know who she is or what she has done with the last few years of her life. But I know she isn't going to be alone before she leaves on that rocket ship for another planet.

I take a step closer and grab her hand. Her skin feels

sticky and cool. It's the skin of a dying person. I lean in and whisper into her ear. "It's okay, Grandma. I'm here. It's Charlie. Remember me?"

"Charlie?" she mumbles. I can barely make it out, but she says my name.

My heart flutters, and I can't believe she's still kind of conscious. "Yeah, Grandma."

In the lowest, softest voice, but somewhat garbled, she says, "I love you."

My eyes fill with tears. I squeeze her hand more tightly. "I love you too, Grandma. I love you so much. And I don't want you to leave me."

Again in the same quiet, low voice she says, "It's time. I've been a great big burden."

"No, Grandma, that's not true."

"You're the only one who's been here for me. I'll never be able to repay you for that. Except to say that I'll always watch over you, Charlie. Even gone, I'll be here for you. Keep chasing your UFOs."

I can't help the tears. Her eyes have yet to open, and her breathing becomes a series of quick short breaths.

"I will, Grandma. I will."

"Who are you talking to?" I look over and see the nurse standing in the doorway. "Sometimes I think they're completely gone, and other times I think they can hear us."

"She was just talking to me."

The nurse looks at me with pity and nods. "Then you just experienced a miracle, because between the morphine and her own body, she's out cold. At least she's not experiencing any pain."

"You mean there's no way she could be awake?"

He shakes his head. "No way. I'm going to try your dad again." He leaves and walks down the hall.

I look over to my grandma, who smiles at me, her eyes still closed. She grips my hand more tightly, and I hold on as she goes on the last ride of her life.

# THE NEW TRUCK RIDE

·····

The weird thing about life is that it doesn't ever plan itself very well. In fact, I think the universe is against plans. "Plans?" it says. "Who needs 'em?" Except, us humans tend to run with plans. And I had one for today, before my grandma died.

I have been saving work money and Tickles walking money and birthday and Christmas money so that I can buy my very own truck.

At 2:00 p.m., I walk to the guy's house.

At 2:24 p.m., I'm sitting in my new 1975 GMC Sierra pickup truck. It's gray with black trim, and it's mine. I'm driving to pick up Seth. He knows all of the news, so I'm hoping things don't get awkward.

Seth comes out of his house when he sees me pull up. I get out of the truck, leaving the door open. He nods. "Look at this baby."

"What do you think?"

"I like it."

The truck isn't much to look at. The wheel wells are

slightly rusted. It has dents and scrapes. But it runs. Or chugs, actually. Kind of coughs, too.

But it's mine.

Susan walks out of the house. "Oh, Charlie." She walks up to me and takes me into her arms. She smells so kind and warm and motherly, like fresh-baked cookies and candles and lavender laundry detergent all rolled into one sweet smell.

She rubs my back. "You poor boy."

Seth takes a deep breath. "Are you sure you want me to go with you?"

I break away from Susan's grasp and wipe my eyes and then nod. "I need you there with me."

As I'm driving, he says, "I'm really sorry about your grandma."

"Can we not talk about that today? I mean, there's nothing to say. She fell asleep and never woke up. Probably had no idea what even happened to her."

Seth reaches out and briefly rubs my shoulder. He's been more touchy as of late, which is sort of annoying, but I haven't said anything.

"What do you want to talk about?" he asks.

"Nothing," I say.

I look over and see Seth fidgeting with his thumbs, and I think of my grandma. After a few seconds he looks over at me and smirks.

I look at him and then back to the road. Then back to him. He's smirking at me, and I can't help but smirk back.

He laughs, and then I join in.

Soon we're laughing as I drive around town. Past old houses and more old houses and a few newer houses. None too big, none fancy.

"Truck works pretty well for being so old," I say.

He nods.

I watch the road and feel the truck bump and bounce along. "Aren't you going to say anything?" I ask.

"Oh. Am I allowed to talk?"

"Actually, now that you mention it, no. This is kind of nice. You just have to listen to me."

Seth nods and purses his lips shut.

I smile.

Not seconds later, Seth says, "Screw it. I'm going to talk."

I look over to him. "That didn't take long."

"Funny," he says dryly. "So we're driving in your new truck on the day your grandma died."

We hit a bump.

Seth continues, "Have you ever noticed that the things we do after someone's death—particularly the little things—have such tremendous importance and power? Almost like it's a statement to the universe saying, 'I'm still alive. Feel my impact.' Like, you'll probably remember everything about this truck ride years in the future."

I pull the truck over to the side of the highway, and turn to him, mouth slightly agape.

"What?" he says.

"When did you become so philosophical?"

Seth chuckles. "Let's just say I have a smart friend who has started to influence me."

I smile. I put the truck into gear, and it sputters off down the road, and we continue our drive as we pass the tiny town of Waterloo.

We both wave, but don't stop.

# SURVIVOR SOUNDS

·····

Geoffrey isn't on his couch when I walk into his house. I actually have to take a moment to look around and make sure I'm in the right place. It's been ages since I haven't seen him on his green love seat.

"Geoffrey? You here?"

I hear music coming from the back of the house, and I head in that direction.

"Geoffrey?"

I see a large man sitting on a bed with a record player near him. A bunch of records are scattered on the bed and the floor.

"Charlie!"

"You're up!"

"I am," he says, and smiles. "I can do some walking again. Never felt so free."

I am amazed at Geoffrey's progress. He doesn't look much different, but he's moving. That's definitely something. "So, what are you doing in here?"

"Listening to some old music. Did you know I used to be in a band?"

"Really?"

I see Tickles lying in the corner of the room, curled up. "Hi, Tickles." He stands up and wags his tail.

"Yep. Back in high school and college. I actually was the singer. Some people said I had the voice of a young Dean Martin."

"Who?"

Geoffrey looks at me like I'm the worst person in the world.

"Sorry to hear about your grandma," he says.

"Thanks. The funeral is on Wednesday, if you can make it."

Geoffrey nods and says, "I'll see what I can do." I'm not sure if he'll be able to make it, and I feel kind of bad for bringing it up, but I figured it would've been rude to not invite him.

There are so many things about Geoffrey that I don't know. I ask him to sing for me.

He laughs and then coughs. "No, no. My pipes aren't what they used to be. Probably full of dust and cobwebs."

"Come on," I nudge.

I think he's considering it. He clears his throat and straightens his back. He begins to sing some song I've never heard before, and he sounds great. Deep voiced, very theatrical. He sings for about thirty seconds and then stops.

I clap. "That was amazing."

"It's something. Now. Can you help me up?"

"Want me to clean up these records?"

"Nah. I'll have Judy do it tomorrow." We slowly make our way to the living room, but Geoffrey is doing most of the work on his own. I'm just guiding him.

I get Geoffrey back to the love seat, and he lowers himself with great effort. He exhales deeply when he gets situated. "Whew." He wipes his brow. "This exercise thing is a bitch."

I laugh. "Oh! You know I just bought a new truck?"

"Is that right? Well, I look forward to the day you take me for a ride."

"Me too," I say. "Me too." And I know it'll happen.

Tickles runs into the room, anxious for his walk.

# THE DAY THE EARTH STANDS STILL

•••••

Things have largely settled down for me. It's funny how so many things can change and yet so many things stay the same. I'm in my familiar room in the same darkened house, but I'm staring out the window, and I sense an awkwardness to searching the Great Beyond for life, to something that used to feel so normal. Ever since school started and my grandma died, I haven't been searching for the UFOs outside my house. I've been focused on chasing the UFOs in my heart. You know, my dreams.

It's Friday night, and Seth is on his way over. I finally agreed to let him see my room. I look around at the piles of dirty clothes, the dishes scattered with crumbs, the mess of Charlie Dickens, and I decide not to clean any of it. And not just because I'm lazy, but because this is me. This is how I am.

There's a knock on the front door, and I hear my dad yell, "Charlie!" He's still largely confined to a chair and a bed. He's watching TV in his bed, so the blue light is now relegated to his bedroom and not the entire house. I don't know if that's good or bad. Though, there's been one great thing to come out of the accident: I haven't seen my dad drink a beer since. He's actually, in a weird way, regaining the life he had before Mom left, as he heals from his fall. He's healing.

Seth is smiling as I open the door. "Here's dinner." He holds a large pizza.

"Yum."

Up the stairs. My heart beats with every step I take.

My bedroom door is closed. My heart thrums. Hands sweaty. Seth stands behind me in the hallway. Not sure what I'm thinking, but I worry he might not like me after he sees my room. Well, I used to worry about that kind of stuff. Now I think that Seth likes me because of me, which is why I finally agreed to let him come over.

"Charlie," he says, "open the door. The box is burning my hands."

The door swings open, and I wait for his first words.

"Hot." He tosses the box of pizza on the bed and blows air on his hand. He looks around at the four walls that so often confine me. "So this is the great Charlie Dickens's bedroom."

I close the door. "Shut up."

"It's nice. I mean, it's a mess, but it's nice."

"Let's just eat. I'm starving."

"Oh. Is that . . ." Seth walks toward the picture that has been freshly hung above my desk.

"It's more beautiful now. I hated your taking it at the time, but I'm so glad you did." I took it home the day she boarded that rocket.

We sit on my bed, and Seth opens the pizza box. "What's the movie tonight?" he asks.

Seth and I recently started watching sci-fi movies and are making our way down the list of the "Greatest Sci-Fi Films of All Time" (at least according to some website).

"It's called *The Day the Earth Stood Still*. It was made in 1951."

"An old one. You know," Seth says, "I'm really turning into a sci-fi fan."

We eat slice after slice of pizza as the movie plays on my laptop. But halfway through this old black-and-white movie, I notice the *Montana UFO Sightings* book on my bookshelf. I can't stop thinking about the sticky note at the back. It's keeping me from enjoying the movie.

Seth notices that I'm distracted while the search is going on for the spaceman. "Something the matter?"

I can't stop thinking about the number. But I can't say anything.

Seth puts down his pizza and pauses the movie. "Charlie, what is it? You can talk to me."

I take a deep breath. "It's—my dad. He told me recently that my mom . . ." I lose my words again; I can't speak. I can't say anything. It feels like my entire world is a lie, and I don't want whatever rocky foundation I've built to come crumbling down. I don't want this fragile house to bury me and Seth when it does come crashing down. I don't want him to decide that I'm too much work, that I'm too messed up.

I look at his eyes, which are pleading for answers. He looks concerned.

"Why hasn't she called? Or fucking emailed? Or even

sent a stupid letter? Why did she let me think that she was taken?"

My body feels like a taught string and if pulled any tighter, I'll snap apart. Done.

"Who? What are you . . . Oh." Seth's eyes flash with understanding.

"What did I do to make her hate me? I thought she was the only one who didn't." I have to stand up because the pain of sitting here, the pressure of the moment, is too great.

"Charlie," says Seth, "you know that's not why. Maybe she's ashamed? Maybe she thought she had let you down and she couldn't handle the guilt? She thought your life would be better without her?"

"He gave me her new phone number. Told me to call her."

"So why don't you?"

"I can't. I couldn't. What would I say?"

"I don't know. Start with 'hi' and go from there."

I feel tears building in my chest and flowing up to my eyes. But I can't sob. I can't cry in front of Seth. I can't . . .

I can't hold the tears back anymore. I slide down the side of my desk to the floor.

Seth comes over, but he doesn't say anything. Instead he reaches out his hands, encouraging me. I put out my hands, and he pulls me up. I'm barely standing before Seth wraps his arms around me.

I feel my foundation crumbling. But he's not letting it bury me. Or him. Or our friendship. I see the picture out of the corner of my eye. We'll help each other up. That's what best friends do.

* * *

Later that night, after saying good-bye to Seth, I notice the blue light coming from my dad's room. Nervously I walk in. I'm not sure what I want to say to him.

"Hey, Charlie. Did I hear crying in your room earlier? I wasn't sure."

I clear my throat. "Ah. Yeah."

"Was it— Did you call your mother?" I see in my father's eyes his genuine interest. His genuine love for me. I feel loved in a way that I haven't felt from him in a long time. But maybe I'm also growing up. Maybe I've lived more experiences and can see that he's loved me all along. Even when it appeared otherwise.

"Not yet," I say. "But—someday."

"Someday is the perfect time." He smiles. Then he says, "And, Charlie, I'm here if you need me. You know that, right? I'll be . . . around more." His eyes fill with tears.

I look at the man in front of me. A man who looks tired, who looks weak, who looks broken. I hate seeing that, so I bend over and hug him as best I can, given that he's in bed.

He chuckles. With a voice full of tears, he asks, "What's this for?"

But I just keep hugging him, and I feel his arms come around me. Then I say, "Thank you, Dad." *Thank you for doing your best. For trying to help me—even if you don't always know how.*

"You're welcome, Charlie."

"Dad?" I say into his chest. "I love you."

He holds me tighter.

The earth stands still.

# THE LAST THING TO SEE

.....

I'm dreading what I'm about to do.

I stare at my phone.

My stomach turns.

I grab my *Montana UFO Sightings* book off the shelf. I open to the back cover and take out the sticky note with the phone number. I deleted my dad's message but wrote the number down just in case I ever had the courage to . . .

Today I woke up with that courage.

I think some things needed to happen before I could try to call. I had to become friends with Seth, and learn that he has my back. I had to witness Geoffrey coming to terms with his own mortality, and have Tickles be my silent adviser through it all. My dad needed to fall and then get back up, and my grandma had to go on her last great journey. I needed to search and find and uncover all the possible aliens around me before I could ever reach out to the ones farther away.

But mostly I needed to find myself. I'll never tell Seth

he was right, but I was too busy looking up and missing out on everything in front of me.

She might have left me, but there are people who have chosen to stay, and they are my family.

With a deep breath I begin to dial her number.

It rings. And rings. I can't stand the anticipation. . . . My head is being crushed under the strain. . . .

"Hello?" she answers, and her voice is as soft as a cloud and as sweet as honey, just like I remembered.

But no memories come flooding back.

"Hello?" she says again.

I have nothing. I'm blank.

"Who is this?" she asks.

I don't know who I am with her.

She's an alien to me.

I hang up and stare out my window. I take a deep breath, and a shooting star sears the crisp Montana night sky. I follow it as it dissipates into nothing, the universe not even remembering that it existed.

The universe is so massive and unforgiving, and it begins to overtake my thoughts, making me feel alone and insignificant, and just when my thoughts begin to overwhelm me, my phone buzzes. . . .

It's Seth. He wants to know if I saw the shooting star. I pick up my phone, thankful that I'm not out there in the Great Beyond, all alone, burning out without a trace. Instead I'm here on earth with people who love me.

I'm home.

# ACKNOWLEDGMENTS

First off, this book would not be in your hands without the indomitable David Gale. This entire journey is because David read my email, asked to look at my novel, and saw the potential in Charlie's story. Thank you, David, for making my dream come true. Thank you, thank you, thank you from the bottom of my heart.

A debt of gratitude goes to my agent Robert Guinsler, who has helped me navigate the open waters of the publishing world. Thank you, Robert, for always having my back and believing in me.

This book would not exist without the amazing team at Simon & Schuster. First off, a big thank you to the publisher, Justin Chanda. Also, thank you to Krista Vossen for a beautifully designed book. Further thanks goes to Tom Daly, Katrina Groover, Martha Hanson, Audrey Gibbons, Lauren Hoffman, Chrissy Noh, Christina Pecorale, Emily Hutton, Michelle Leo, and Sarah Woodruff. A special thank-you goes to Amanda Ramirez, who has been invaluable in helping this book find its way to the world.

Thank you to Matt Saunders who brought a beautiful book cover to life.

*Earth to Charlie* has had many readers since the very first draft back in 2015. A big thank-you to Mandy Haller, Janet Trumble, Brenda Lamb, Andrea Massaro, Natalie Kinsella, Trudy Wood, Tevin Stutzman, and Isabel Galupo for reading Charlie's story, providing helpful notes, and giving encouragement along the way. This book wouldn't be where it is today without you.

Thank you to Matt Sadeghian and Amy Schiffman, for championing this novel in the world of Hollywood.

To the Novel19s group—thank you for your support! I have made so many friends with you amazing writers, and I hope that our friendship continues beyond our debut year.

There have been many people in my life who have championed my writing and who have taken the time to read my earlier novels. The support you have given me throughout the years has gotten me to this point. I sincerely thank each and every one of you. It means the world.

Not going to lie, I had given up on getting this book published after 50+ agent rejections. Charlie's story was going to quickly make its bed with the four other novels I had finished and couldn't get repped. But then Jerell Rosales read it and loved it enough to say, "Keep sending it out. Get to one hundred rejections." His words gave me the needed boost to restart the long and arduous querying process. But this time it worked! So a big fat hearty thank-you goes to Jerell for his unwavering support in this book. Our many talks and your continued support means so much to me.

June Severance has guided my writing since way back when I was writing screenplays. I would not be the writer I am today without our many conversations over tea and your hand-written notes. I know you'd be proud of this novel.

To all my friends, thank you for being by my side as we navigate this thing called life.

To all my family, thank you for your unwavering support. (This includes my grandparents, Jack and Nancy Datres, and Arnold and Shirley Olson, whom I still deeply miss.) Also, a special shout-out to my brother, Jake, who has read this book and many of my others—making time even with his busy life in the world of science.

Thank-you to the many librarians and booksellers— the real warriors of the book world—for championing this novel.

I can't forget to thank Yossarian. He won't read this, but he's been a great writing buddy. He keeps my world light-hearted and the journey interesting.

I would be lost without my parents, who have supported my writing habit throughout the nearly thirteen years it took to get here. They've always believed in me, even if they were concerned when I would stare at the laptop for too long. (These books don't write themselves.) Dale and Trudi Olson are the best parents I could have ever asked for. Thank you for all your love and all your support.

Finally, thank you, dear reader, for picking up my debut novel. If you're still reading these acknowledgements, then I'm guessing you probably liked my book (if not, what are you doing here?! Just kidding). I would be so honored if you could share or recommend Charlie's story to other people in person or online. After all, any book's success depends on readers like you supporting it. Also, while I've got your attention, support your local bookstores. Nothing beats browsing bookshelves and stumbling across something that has the potential to light up your life; and frankly, I find the prospect of no physical bookstores the beginning of a dystopian world. (Is that a new novel idea?)

I think that's it. Though now I'm nervous I forgot someone, and if I did, know that it wasn't intentional. I'm just scatterbrained and trying to write a new book. Well, my coffee's gone, so I'm going to wrap this up right here. Until next time.